BY BRUCE CLEMENTS

Two Against the Tide (1967)

The Face of Abraham Candle (1969)

From Ice Set Free: The Story of Otto Kiep (1972)

I Tell a Lie Every So Often (1974)

Coming Home to a Place You've Never Been Before
*with Hanna Clements* (1975)

Prison Window, Jerusalem Blue (1977)

Anywhere Else But Here (1980)

Coming About (1984)

The Treasure of Plunderell Manor (1987)

Tom Loves Anna Loves Tom (1990)

A Chapel of Thieves (2002)

# A Chapel of Thieves

# A Chapel of Thieves

## BRUCE CLEMENTS

FARRAR, STRAUS AND GIROUX

NEW YORK

Library of Congress Cataloging-in-Publication Data

Clements, Bruce.

A chapel of thieves / Bruce Clements.— 1st ed.

p. cm.

Summary: In 1849, Henry, a resourceful young man, sets off from Missouri to Paris in hopes of saving his older brother, a self-styled preacher, from the clutches of a clever charlatan.

ISBN 0-374-37701-4

[1. Brothers—Fiction.   2. Voyages and travels—Fiction.   3. Paris (France)—Fiction.]   I. Title.

PZ7.C5912 Ch 2002

[Fic]—dc21

2001046030

*To Enzo, book lover*

# A CHAPEL OF THIEVES

## WHAT THIS BOOK IS ABOUT

This book tells what happened when I went to Paris in 1849 to rescue my brother, Clayton, from a Chapel full of thieves. In it you will meet Dr. Alexandre Gelineau, who can amputate a man's foot in the street and spill less than a cup of blood; his sister Cécile, who can knock down a kidnapper with a chair leg; Deacon George, who loves to do evil and make others take the blame; Victor Hugo, a great writer who can draw a crowd and start a riot any time he pleases; and Le Furet, which is French for "The Ferret," who can slide through a crowd with a sack of stolen goods on his shoulder, and nobody the wiser.

Deacon George put Clayton in danger, and Dr. Gelineau, Cécile, Ferret, and Mr. Hugo got him out of it. Without those four, I would now be sitting in a cell in the Saint-Lazare Prison, with no pencil, no paper, and not much hope.

My brother is a serious man. He has no time for games, or toys, or other people's ideas. Even his jokes are serious. One night when I was five and he was nine he came into my room with a dead rabbit and woke me up. The rabbit's name was Lazarus, he said, in honor of the man Jesus raised from the dead. He was going to take him out into the garden at midnight, pray him back to life, feed him some fresh lettuce, carry him back upstairs, and put him on my bed, and the next morning when I woke up, I would be able to play with him.

When I woke up, Lazarus was lying on my pillow, but he was still dead, and Clayton was standing next to the window. He had prayed him back to life, he said, and fed him his lettuce, and brought him into my room, and put him on my pillow, but I had rolled over on him in my sleep and killed him all over again. I started to cry and carry on, and Clayton hugged me and patted my shoulder and told me to be quiet, he was just testing to see if I had True Faith.

"It's true I prayed him back to life," he said, "but five minutes later he died from a sudden attack of pneumonia."

I was glad I hadn't killed the little bunny, but I was sad that he would never again be able to frolic with his friends. It made me think about what it is that makes us alive. Mama thought about that a lot, too. Whenever a lady in our church had a new baby, Mama would say, "The Spark of Life has arrived," and whenever somebody died, she'd say, "The Spark of Life has gone." I heard her say "Spark of Life" so many times, I thought it was one word.

After breakfast, Clayton said that if I came out into the back yard and helped him give Lazarus a decent funeral, he would give me a nutty surprise. While I was digging the grave, he told me how important it was to bury all the parts of a body in one spot.

"When Judgment Day comes," he said, "all the men who lost body parts in this life, legs cut off by locomotives, ears bitten off in fights, limbs shot off by cannons, eyes pecked out by birds, and so forth, and didn't hold on to them, are going to have to run around collecting these parts before they can stand up whole before the Lord to get their selves judged."

"What if one of his parts was blown to bits, or a dog found it and ate it?" I asked him.

"If you have the True Faith, Henry, you will find your missing parts no matter how bitty the bits are. That's why I keep all my hair cuttings and fingernail pairings in a sack in the cellar. You can't be too careful when it comes to Judgment Day."

While I was reaching down into the hole to pry out a rock, I asked him what "Sparkalife" was.

"Henry, you are a two-times-over fool," he said. "First off, it's three words, not one, and second, that hole needs to be twice as deep as it is."

While I worked with the shovel again, he preached me a sermon about what happens when the Spark of Life goes out of a man who's got no religion. "Satan snatches that man's soul, draws it down to his Dark Kingdom, and throws it onto his Eternal Fire, where it sizzles for all eternity," he said. "Of course, rabbits don't have souls. We're just being careful with this one for practice and because it is an example of a miraculous rising."

After the funeral I asked him for my nutty surprise, and he picked up a rotten acorn and gave it to me. "Plant this in the ground," he said, "and if you grow an oak tree out of it, it'll be the nuttiest surprise ever."

That night I dreamed I was standing next to the red-hot door of Hell with Oingo, our dog, trying to get her to go home before Satan came out and grabbed both of us. She'd run off and go around the corner, or she would just disappear the way dogs do, and I would think she was gone, but then all of a sudden she would be back again. I didn't have many bad dreams when I was little. That one was the worst.

Warning people against sin has always been Clayton's favorite work. According to Mama, "sin" was the first word he ever spoke. To this day, his favorite Bible subject is "Shady Ladies in Scripture." He loves to tell the stories of the evil deeds of these females. He has three favorites: "Sinful Seductive Salome," who danced in front of King Herod and made him chop off John the Baptist's head and bring it to her on a silver platter; "Devilish Defiled Delilah," who got Samson into her tent, cut off all his hair, and kept him as her slave; and "Jealous Jade Jezebel," who had more blazing romances than a dog has fleas. Telling their stories makes him grin, caper about, and clap his hands.

The only thing in the Bible Clayton doesn't like is the foreign words. "Foreign words is like chiggers," he says. "They get into your eyes and crawl back into your brain and turn it into offal. It's the Devil behind all foreign languages." He hates French most of all.

Still, it was France he went to when he grew up. Strange.

## II

## WHY CLAYTON CHOSE TO GO TO FRANCE

Since Clayton hates all foreign words, not to mention foreigners, why did he want to go to France? There were five reasons:

1) His heart was broken.

2) He thought I was making fun of him.

3) He knew Aunt Minna was sick, and that as soon as she died, Mama and Papa were going to leave Saint Louis and go take over her farm, and he wanted to leave them behind before they left him behind.

4) I already had a job, at Mr. Henze's Funeral Parlor, where I slept nights, and he had no job and was still sleeping at home.

5) An Angel in a dream told him to go.

The biggest reason was Number One. Here is how his heart got broken:

In the summer of 1848, he and I went up the Missouri River to try to rescue our little cousin Hanna from kidnappers. That trip turned out to be such an adventure that I wrote a book about it when we got home, which I called *I Tell a Lie Every So Often*. My idea was to find a company in New York that would print it and give me ten cents on the dollar for every copy they sold, which is the common way in the book business.

Before I decided on a company to send it to, Clemmy Burke, Clayton's Intended Bride, came to me and asked me if she could read it. (Clemmy was his second choice. At first he wanted to marry her sister, Caroline, but he began to worry she might be too flat-chested for his taste, so he had switched to Clemmy.) She kept it a week, and when she got to the chapter near the end where Clayton loses his pants in public, she got so disgusted she stomped over to our house, stood in the middle of our front yard, and dared Clayton and me to come out and face her.

As soon as we came out, she threw his engagement ring on the ground and kicked it under the porch, and threw all my pages up into the air. She had a strong arm, so they went high up and came down like snow. Then she looked at me and shook her fist.

"Henry Desant," she said, "you are a Demon from the Burning Pit of Eternal Fire. When you die, which will happen right now if there is any justice in the world, you will be hauled by your fingernails with burning-hot tongs before the Judgment Seat of God, and He will bind you hand and foot and send you to the Red-Hot Place of Eternal Punishment, where you will roast for all eternity, world without end, amen, and it serves you right. What do you think of that?"

She was standing there with her arms folded across her

chest, tapping her foot in the mud, which made a squishy, slapping noise. I didn't know what to say to her, but I knew she was waiting for me to say *something*. "It seems like a lot of trouble to go to," I said, "the tongs and the binding up and all, just for my benefit."

"That's exactly the sort of thing you would think, Henry, but God will not be mocked, no siree, Bob, and no more will I."

She stomped onto the porch and backed Clayton up against the front door. "It's a shame, Mr. Clayton Desant, that you've got yourself a brother like Henry tied around your neck like an albacore on a rope. But, sorry as I am for you, I cannot allow myself to be united into the Bonds of Holy Matrimony with a man who has appeared in his undergarments in print. I therefore bid you farewell forever."

She turned around and went down the porch steps and stomped to the front gate. Oingo was sitting next to it, waiting to be petted, and got up wagging her tail, but Clemmy kicked at her and then turned around and pointed her finger at me. "One other thing, Henry. You keep your filthy, swaybacked South Seas mongrel out of my way at all times."

Oingo didn't understand all of Clemmy's words, but she was shocked by her tone of voice and skittered over to me for comfort.

I was shocked, too. All readers have the right to criticize books. Criticism, when offered in a charitable spirit, is bound to make a good writer better. Going so far as to criticize Oingo was something else again. It was mean, and it showed that Clemmy knew nothing about dogs. It's true Oingo is a mongrel, being half Siberian and half poodle, but mongrels are the best and most faithful dogs in the world. Oingo's first master was a riverfront slave who had been crushed between a dock and a lumber barge. On the afternoon of his funeral, I had to hold on to Oingo to keep her from jumping into his grave. After that she starved herself for a week, and for a month more she would only eat if you took her on your lap and fed her by hand.

She had no part in writing the book, except for sometimes jumping on me, or pushing against me, or barking, to make me put down my pencil and play with her.

After Clemmy was out of sight, Clayton looked at me and said, "So, Henry, how does it feel to be the Snake in the Garden?"

"I'm sorry," I said.

"There's no call for you mocking me in my misery, Henry," he said. "Now neither sister will marry me, and it's all your fault and I will never trust you again."

Since he had never trusted me before, it was not such a loss, but still I was sorry.

We had a family of coons living under the porch. Coons love to hoard gold and glass, so I climbed under there right away to find Clayton's ring. Oingo was already under, digging and sniffing. I found the ring, rubbed off the dirt, backed out, and gave it to Clayton. He was ready to take it from me, but he wasn't ready to shake my hand and say thank you.

When he needs to brood, Clayton eats dinner alone. That night he took his dinner and his Bible out onto the back porch. After he had finished three helpings of pork with corn mush, half a loaf of bread, two slices of raisin pie, and ten chapters of the Book of Leviticus, washed down with a quart of milk, he went straight up to his room and flopped on his bed and fell asleep. As soon as he started snoring, Mama went upstairs, took off his shoes, and put a blanket over him.

In the middle of the night he had a dream. He was standing in the front yard, and a high carriage pulled by six white horses came down the street and stopped in front. The driver blew a trumpet and opened the door, and the Angel Gabriel stepped out. He had on a soldier's uniform, with a Napoleon hat on his head and a sword hanging from a golden belt. He came over to our gate and looked Clayton in the eye and said, "Leave these children of Eve behind, cross the Great Ocean, and preach in the Dark City where the greatest sinners are."

Then he threw a fistful of gold coins up into the air. As soon as Clayton was finished picking them up, Gabriel reached inside his shirt and pulled out a gold goblet full of water, dropped in a handful of bicarbonate of soda, and told him to drink it. When Clayton had swallowed the last swallow, he woke up. It was pitch-dark, and he could taste the bicarbonate on his lips, which was proof to him that his dream had been a Divine Revelation. He stayed awake the rest of the night, belching and meditating on the Divine Command, and when he came downstairs for breakfast the next morning he wasn't bloated anymore and had a big smile on his face.

"Mama and Papa," he said, "I have received the Divine Call. I am on my way to Paris, France, to wrestle with the Devil and harvest the souls of great sinners. No no no, don't try to talk me out of it. I am going to rent a Chapel in the middle of the city, put a sign up in front with my name on it, and preach night and day, just like Jonah did after the Whale spit him out on the shore of Nineveh. The worst sinners will come to me to be saved, and I will be known far and wide as the Tonsils of the Lord."

Papa reminded him that he had wolfed down his dinner the night before, including two big wedges of raisin pie, and then had gone to bed with all that food on his stomach. "Don't buy your boat ticket right away," he said. "Think it over a few days. It might have been the Angel Gabriel in your dream, but it might have been gas, too. You know how raisin pie always puffs you up."

Clayton took a deep breath and shook his head. "This is a one hundred percent genuine Spiritual Matter, Papa, just like it was with Jonah and the Whale. The man who is standing before you now in this humble kitchen is the chosen Messenger of God, ready to go jaw to jaw against the Evil Powers and Potentates and Principalities of this world. It's not everyone can fight in that battle, but I am one of those who can, you see if I'm not. The Divine Light has come to me, and the Divine Voice has knocked upon my door. Jonah's Destiny was clear to him when the Whale spit him up on Nineveh, and mine is clear to me now, even though I ain't never been swallowed even once."

There was no use trying to stop him. We could only hope that the Angel Gabriel would appear to him in another dream and tell him to stay home and find a job. Right after breakfast he went to the bank and took out five hundred dollars, which was his half of the one thousand dollars Aunt

Minna gave us boys when she died. To this he added various dribs and drabs of money, from birthdays and such, and two days later we were all on the steamboat dock waving goodbye to him as he sailed out into the river on his way to New Orleans to catch a ship for France.

## III

## WHY CLAYTON CHOSE PARIS
## OVER ALL OTHER CITIES

Clayton picked Paris over all the other cities in the world because of what happened to him on his seventh birthday. With Mama downstairs fixing breakfast and Papa in the back shaving, he went into their room and began hunting around for his present. On the top shelf of their closet he found a tin box full to the top with Fruit Jellies, with a picture of the Champ-de-Mars, which is a Paris horseracing park, on the lid. He carried the box outside behind the shed and sat there studying the picture, which had ladies with parasols, and carriages, and flags blowing in the wind, and men cheering their favorite horses, and all the while he was eating the jellies. When he was done he came back inside, told Mama he didn't want any breakfast, and threw up on the kitchen floor. I was only three years old, but I still remember the colorful vomit. It was like a stirred-up rainbow.

It doesn't take much to make Clayton sick, but he gets better quick, too. The next day he went up and down the street knocking on doors and warning people never to eat sweets made in Paris because it was an Evil City where they ate horseflesh and made dark perfumes for Shady Ladies by boiling up funeral flowers.

He ate alone that night, and when Saturday rolled around he took his birthday dollar and went downtown and bought some American jelly beans and twenty little paper sacks. I drew an American flag on each sack, and he made twenty little piles of beans and poured the piles into the sacks. Then he went all over the neighborhood selling the sacks door-to-door for a dime apiece, telling his customers they were sweet and healthy both, not like French candies, which turned good people into monsters.

When he got back home, he had two dollars in his pocket in place of the one he had started out with. So four things got permanently hooked together in his mind: God, Sin, Paris, and doubling your money.

IV

## THE LETTER WHICH STARTED
## ME ON THIS ADVENTURE

When you get a letter from Clayton, it's like he's talking right in your ear. Important words he writes in capital letters with lines under them, and big ideas he finishes off with exclamation points. Also, he loves asking questions with many question marks.

Here is the letter I received from him on March 5, 1849:

*Dear Henry!*

*Are you sitting down in a chair?? Better do!! HERE IS MY GREAT NEWS: I have won a CONGREGATION OF TRUE BELIEVERS. Fifteen men came to my Chapel with offerings on January the First and repented of all of their sins!! What do you think of that????*

*Before that Great New Year's Day, like all true prophets, I was a lonesome voice in this sinful city, with no one to hear me preach but drunkards and dirty riffraff children.*

But did I lose heart????? <u>NO!!!!</u> I fought on, and my reward is getting *A TRUE AND FAITHFUL FLOCK* listening to me and bringing offerings every night.

My Chapel was once just a low tavern, a den of drunkards and <u>SHADY LADIES</u>, and we have not yet got rid of the tavern stink from those former days, but that stench is now *A Righteous Reek* in the nostrils of God Tuesday through Friday nights plus Sunday mornings, and my heart rejoices!!

I must give due credit to the man who led these sinners to me. He is my *FAITHFUL DEACON*, George Goric, a Polish Prince who was driven from his homeland by his wicked younger brother, and now serves me and God.

Deacon George knows *TWO THOUSAND AND FIVE HUNDRED ENGLISH WORDS*. Four nights a week, plus Sundays, he stands faithfully by my side turning my sermons into French. After the last Amen he sends my flock out into the streets of this Dark City, and gets people to give them silk, silver, ivory, and small pieces of furniture. These items he sells, and then he uses the money to help the poor. All the work I need to do is study my Bible, preach, and keep a record of the offerings in a Book Deacon George has given me.

Late every night my flock returns with their offerings, and I sit at my desk in our "Upper Room" with my pencil and my <u>LEATHER BOUND RECORD BOOK</u>, writing down each item of our night's "harvest."

*It's the Bible Story of the Prodigal Son all over again, except that this time it is the Elder Brother (ME), who goes into a far country and takes it by storm, winning countless sinners to his side, while the younger brother (YOU) sits at home burying the dead!!*

*You must go to Clemmy's house the very day you get this letter and tell her what a GREAT SUCCESS I am here, how much my true believers love me and hang on to my every word. Then she will see that scorning a Good Man (ME) is like <u>cutting off your nose in spite of your voice</u>. And do not fail to give my kindest regards and blessings to her Dear Family, and do it right now!!!*

*Your Elder Brother,*
*CLAYTON*

As soon as I read the letter, I knew I had to quit my job at Henze's Funeral Parlor and go to Paris and try to pry my brother loose from Deacon George and that chapel of thieves. The odds were against me. Clayton never has taken my advice. Nobody likes to admit that he has blinded himself to what is right in front of his eyes.

## ABOUT MAKING YOURSELF BLIND

I t's easy to make yourself blind. You see something you don't want to see, so you turn your head and look the other way. I used to do that all the time with slaves. They were everywhere in Saint Louis, doing all kinds of jobs, unloading boats, driving wagons, washing windows, and looking after rich white children, but most days I paid no attention to them.

Sometimes I *had* to pay attention, of course. If I was walking by a stable yard and saw a whipping, or looked across the street and saw a little sister being torn away from her brother, or went with Mr. Henze to pick up a slave's body, which we did about once a month because we were the only people who wanted the business, and the body was bruised and bloody, or had chain marks, my eyes would be open for a day or two, and I would remember all the other terrible crimes I had heard about, such as masters branding their slaves to punish them or keep them from running away, or killing them and throwing their bodies in the river, and I would be ashamed of being white and free.

Pretty soon, however, I would let myself go blind again. So it was easy for me to see how Clayton could do the same thing, closing his eyes and studying his Bible and preaching his sermons as if he had a Chapel full of honest men. He didn't want to see they were thieves, so he didn't.

Sometimes, it can help you to be blind. If you're sick, but you don't have money for a doctor, or if you have a hateful job, but you can't quit, blindness is best. Clayton was in a different boat, however. He was running a hideout for pickpockets, housebreakers, and snatch-and-run jewelry thieves, and "Deacon George" was making him keep a list, in his own handwriting, of everything they stole, so if they got caught, it would look as if he was the brains of the gang.

Some night soon, a squad of policemen was going to walk into his Chapel and find him standing in front holding a Bible in one hand and a dozen stolen forks in the other. They would arrest him right away as a Master Thief, take him away to prison, throw him in a cold dark cell, and leave him there to live on bread and water. Then, if the rats didn't bite him and give him blood poisoning first, the Prosecutor would bring him before a Judge, and Deacon George would stand up in the witness box and say he was an American bandit from the Wild West leading innocent Frenchmen into a life of crime. And all the while Clayton would sit there not even knowing what the man was saying, and after ten minutes the Judge would bang down his gavel and send him to prison.

And I might not be able to help him. What was I but just another American who couldn't speak the language? I could even make things worse for Clayton instead of better. So I decided I would learn as much French as I could on the way there. It was a long trip, six or seven or eight days down the Mississippi, and then four or five weeks on the ship across the Atlantic. Knowing I had to keep my brother out of prison would prod me to study hard, so when I got there I would at least be able to understand some few simple things.

Mr. John Milton, the famous poet, now dead, says that if he ever were to start a school, he would teach the boys Italian, Latin, Greek, and Hebrew all at the same time. I'm not nearly as smart as Mr. Milton's boys would have been, but I had only one language to learn, so I figured I would surely get at least *some* French into my head by the time I got over there. People are good at heart, so I knew that if I stopped on a Paris street and asked a Frenchman for directions, he'd talk slowly and tell me how to get where I wanted to go.

I had a leather money pouch with two pockets to hang around my neck under my shirt. I went to the bank and took out my five hundred dollars from Aunt Minna and put ten ten-dollar gold pieces in the button-down side, and four hundred dollars in paper money in the pocket that tied with a string.

Then I wrote a letter to Clayton telling him I had opened up the back of Aunt Minna's broken mantelpiece clock and found four hundred dollars clogging up the works, and I was coming to Paris right away to give him his half. If Deacon George read the letter, which was almost a sure thing, he would think about that two hundred dollars and start to take special care of Clayton until I got there.

The clock part was a lie, of course, which meant I would have to give up two hundred dollars out of my money, but that was a cheap enough price if the promise of it helped keep him safe for a while. And if I ran out of money in Paris, I knew two trades, undertaking, which I had learned from Mr. Henze, and coopering, which I had learned from my father. People die just as much in France as anywhere else, and with all that wine, they need to fix barrels all the time, so one way or another I would find a job if I was broke.

After I mailed the letter, I went to a store selling old books and bought a French Bible with maps of Egypt and the Holy Land in the back, drawn at the time of Napoleon's War there, and a brand new French-English Dictionary. I already knew the story of Adam and Eve, some Psalms, the Sermon on the Mount, the Lord's Prayer, and the Christmas story, more or less by heart, so if I read them to myself in French I would have the English words running through my head at the same time. At five dollars for the pair, it was a bargain.

Then, to make sure I'd have a place on board, I went and got my boat ticket down the river as far as New Orleans.

VI

## MY FIRST IDEAS ABOUT PARIS

We used to have a calendar on our kitchen wall at home printed by the Missouri Central Railroad, with the title in golden letters, "Three Great Cities of the World." There were pink clouds and Angels at the top, and the ocean with whales jumping at the bottom, and in between bird's-eye views of London, Saint Louis, and Paris. Saint Louis was in the middle and took up the most room, but Paris had the most things to see. The year I learned that there were more numbers than I had fingers, I used to get up on a chair and count the bridges across the Seine River, which slid through the city like a fat blue snake. There were twenty-five of them. That seemed to me like a lot of bridges, but Paris is eight hundred years old, so it only amounts to about three a century.

The more I thought back on it, the more sure I was that Paris would be a lot like Saint Louis. Saint Louis isn't yet fifty years old, with buildings going up and getting torn down all the time, and there are no monuments to speak of, and half the people are just passing through on their way somewhere else, while old Paris has stone arches, cathedrals, a King and Queen, and more than a hundred thousand people who were born there and would never want to live anywhere else. *Still*, like Saint Louis, it would have blacksmiths, and bakeries, and butcher shops, and farmers coming in every morning to sell their goods, and carriages on the streets day and night, and ships and docks and warehouses and taverns.

The rich people in both places would live in the rich sections, with big houses and flower gardens and servants going to and fro, and the not-so-rich people would live in the middling sections, with one-horse traps, and small houses, and vegetable gardens, and not many servants, and the poor people would live in the poor sections, with falling-down houses and filthy streets full of drunks, day laborers, rag-and-bone buyers, cripples, and children.

Clayton always thought it was a good idea keeping different sorts of people apart. Slaves and free, Christians and everybody else, Americans and foreigners, rich and poor, and good and bad. He had a dream once where he had to separate the good people from the bad ones, pinning tags on them so God would know which group to send to the fiery pit. "People like to be with people they feel like they're like," he'd say. "If you put a bad man in heaven he'd just pine away for his friends in the other place. The sooner people get put where they belong, the better."

Clayton's idea was to ship all the different people somewhere else—west, or back east, or over to Europe where they came from. Mr. Henze and I gave funerals for a lot of people from Europe whose relatives went home as soon as the funeral was over. He would try to get them to put off buying their tickets until the first shock was over, especially if they had children, but most of them couldn't wait to leave.

In Paris the poor people had nowhere to go, so when they couldn't abide the misery anymore, they would riot, build barricades out of old tables and broken wagons and brass beds and bags of ashes, and wait for the soldiers to come with cannons to blast the barricades down. Some would take out their old guns and shoot, and the rest would throw stones at the soldiers, or pour boiling water and filth down from their windows until they had to surrender.

During the year before, 1848, Paris had been boiling over with revolution. Poor people had taken over the streets, built barricades, and fought against the Army and the police. When it was all over, one thousand five hundred poor men and women and children were dead, and five thousand more had been shipped off to Algeria, in North Africa, where they couldn't start any more trouble, at least not any that you would notice in Paris.

## I TELL MR. HENZE I AM LEAVING

Mr. Henze never made enough profit to put somebody on the payroll who already knew the funeral business. He had hired me for two reasons. First, I was cheap. Second, it was cholera season, and he didn't have time to look for somebody older who had done that kind of work before.

Now he was going to have to find somebody just as ignorant as I had been. It would be hard. Undertaking isn't the kind of work every Tom, Dick, and Harry cares to do. You have to want to help people, the living as well as the dead, and the hours can be queer. It's like being a fireman or an actor. You get busy times, when you're working day and night, and slack times, when you have nothing to do but polish the coffins and play cards.

As soon as I had my books and my ticket, I went to Mr. Henze's office and showed him Clayton's letter. "It's my fault he went to France in the first place," I said. "I made him lose his Intended Bride, which broke his heart and drove him away, so I have to go help him as quick as quick can be."

"Clemmy Burke? Is she the one?"

"Yes, Sir."

"I know her. He'll thank you someday."

"With all due respect, Sir, I don't think so."

"You know best. But you can't just write your papa and mama and say you're going. You have to go tell them yourself, and give them a chance to talk you out of it."

I already had my ticket for the next day, but I promised him I would trade it in and go to Aunt Minna's farm to see Mama and Papa.

He was satisfied at that, and proceeded to give me good advice about places that cater to strangers, especially hotels and restaurants. Whenever I got to one or the other, he said, I had to go look at the privy first. If it was clean, then the bedsheets and the plates and the knives and forks would probably be clean, too. I thanked him for the tip.

He said I would always have a job with him if I came back and wanted one. After that he brought me to the closet, took out my funeral suit, complete with shirt, tie, and studs, and put it in a leather satchel with straps and a lock, and gave the whole kit to me. "The suit's already too tight on you, but I know I won't find anybody else as skinny, so you might as well have the use left in it, and the satchel owner ain't traveling anymore," he said.

Then we sat down at his desk and played our last games of rummy and blackjack.

## I GO TO CLEMMY'S AND
## BOAST FOR CLAYTON

After dinner, I went to Clemmy Burke's house to boast for Clayton. She was sitting on her porch with a new beau, Mr. Savoy Prue, drinking sarsaparilla and eating toast ends.

"Mr. Savoy Prue, Mr. Henry Desant," she said. "Looka-here, Henry, this Mr. Prue is a genuine railroad Surveyor."

He stood up and shook my hand and sat back down. Clemmy poked a piece of toast in his mouth. "This dear man has taken to paying calls on me every chance he gets, Henry, which amounts to three or four times a week. Mr. Prue is one of the most important men now employed by the Missouri Central Railroad. Every train in the State would be down in the ditch if it wasn't for him."

"I'm only a Surveyor," Mr. Prue said.

She leaned against him. "Why, Mr. Savoy Prue, I do believe you have let the wax in your ears get so thick-packed you can't hear good anymore. Cast your mind back to when Henry here clomb onto the porch, and you will recall that I already told him what you are. But you are no plain ordinary everyday Surveyor. When you are done drawing your pretty little drawings, you hold them up in front of the common day laborers and say, 'Put this here bridge right over there by that rosebush,' and even if they can't speak a word of English, which most of them can't, half of them being Chinee and the Good Lord only knows what the rest are, they put it just where you tell them and nowhere else, and the trains go rolling across as pretty as you please."

Mr. Prue sat there blushing and shaking his head.

She poked him with her elbow and looked at me. "Now, I want Savoy to hear about your sweet little waggy-tailed doggie, Henry. Henry has the world's most adorable puppy dog, Mr. Prue. Cunning cunning cunning! He's just a weentsy bit swaybacked, and he doesn't care who he makes up to, but he swam the entire way across the salty ocean from the South Seas to get here. I swan, he's as cute as a bug's ear."

"Oingo's a lady, and she isn't from the South Seas," I said.

Clemmy wagged her finger at me. "Well, of course, she's not from the South Seas any*more*, you silly boy. How could she be, when she's two streets away at your house?"

I didn't want to hear Oingo slandered anymore, and besides, it was time to boast for Clayton.

"Clayton is a big success in Paris," I said.

Clemmy rolled her eyes around. "Mr. Prue, I should warn you that Henry Desant is the biggest liar for a hundred miles around. See his ears going all pink? It's a sure sign."

She was wrong there, too. I never blush when I lie, but I wasn't ready to admit it. I took Clayton's letter out of my pocket so she could see his handwriting on the outside of the envelope. "He told me himself," I said. "He's preaching four times a week, and his True Believers keep coming back for more. I'm going there to see him."

"To Paris?"

"Before the week's over I'm starting."

"The one over there in France?"

"That's where."

"Well, I swan."

Having done my duty by Clayton, I thought I would give Mr. Prue a chance to show how smart and lively he was, so I asked him what was new in railroading. He sat up and took a little pad of paper and a brand-new pencil out of his pocket and started to draw me a sketch of a new kind of switch they had begun to use so the rail yards could be made shorter.

Clemmy began to hum and wiggle around. Then she grabbed his elbow and shook it. When he kept on drawing, she took her fan and knocked his pencil out onto the lawn. While Mr. Prue was crawling around there looking for it, she said, so he could hear, "Now, Henry, you take, for instance, your brother, Clayton. He would never sit on a gracious young lady's front porch drawing foolish pictures when he could be whispering sweet words in her seashell ear, would he, him being a man who goes to foreign parts for spiritual purposes, which is about the bravest and the most noble thing a man can do, don't you think?"

"It depends on his reasons," I said.

"Well, never mind what he would do if he was here amongst us at this moment, I'm sure you will agree that he has been away from us long enough. When, pray tell, is he coming home?"

I took his letter out of the envelope and looked at it as if I was trying to find the answer to her question.

She reached out to grab it. She got the envelope, but I kept hold of the letter.

"I'm going to keep this," she said real loud, looking down at Mr. Prue, who was still crawling in the grass. "It's got his address on. Maybe I'll write him a letter. And maybe I won't. We all miss him something fierce, don't we, Henry? A man like Clayton Desant doesn't come along to bring light and, mayhap, romance into your life every day."

"That's true," I said.

Mr. Prue came back onto the porch with his pencil and pad, and put them away, and Clemmy pushed them deeper down into his pocket.

"What do you think, Mr. Prue? Should I write Henry's brother a letter to faraway France?"

"If you wish it," Mr. Prue said.

"It would fill his heart with joy, I know. Clayton's heart has always been partial to me. I know if I just wrote him a few lines on that nice scented paper he gave me for my birthday, I could have him sitting right here on this porch in a flash, just the way you are now, except he would be all wet and salty from the swim. Ha ha ha! That is merely a joke, of course. A true gentleman like Clayton would get a towel and dry himself off before he came. Ha ha ha again!"

"I think you should write him and tell him you want him to come home," I said.

"Oh? Well, I can't. You want to know why? Because a gracious young lady never begs a gentleman to do anything. It is beneath her dignity to do such."

"Then you probably shouldn't," I said.

"You think I shouldn't? Well, in that case maybe I should. And maybe I will. We'll see. And now I can see that you want to get up and say goodbye to my daddy. He's right out back spading the garden. Goodbye."

I went around into the back garden, where Mr. Burke gave me a lecture about never planting peas in wet ground. Then I said goodbye, went back to the Henzes', and went to bed.

## I TELL MAMA AND PAPA I'M GOING

Having promised Mr. Henze I would go see Mama and Papa before I went to Paris, I traded in my boat ticket and started out for Rocheport. It was four days there and back.

From the outside Aunt Minna's house looked the same as it always had, but inside our furniture was all mixed up with hers, so it looked completely different. Of course, Papa and Mama were the same, and Oingo showed me around the yard as if she had lived there all her life.

I didn't want Papa and Mama to see my letter from Clayton, so I had left it back in Saint Louis. He had sent them one, too, telling about his success, but he had left out the part about his flock going out at night to collect goods.

Mama and Papa didn't want me going across the ocean after him, but they could see I had made up my mind. I only stayed with them one night, with Oingo sleeping on my feet, and then I went back to Saint Louis to catch the next boat to New Orleans.

## WHY I CANNOT EXPECT EVER TO
## MARRY CÉCILE GELINEAU

I thank Mr. Henze for making me visit Mama and Papa on the farm. If I hadn't done that, I would have left Saint Louis four days sooner and missed meeting Dr. Alexandre Gelineau and his sister, Cécile, who have changed my life forever.

Before I tell anything more about them, I must make it plain that I do not have the smallest hope of ever making Cécile my wife. Here is why:

1) She is two years older.

2) She belongs to *La Haute Société*, which means High French Society.

3) She saw her brother murdered in the street, and her grief has purified her soul far above mine.

4) While she has remained pure, I have polluted my soul by gambling and telling lies and receiving stolen goods and desiring the death of my enemy.

For these reasons, therefore, I cannot hope that Cécile and I will ever be husband and wife.

On the other hand, Mama was two years older than Papa when they got married. That, however, was somewhat different. They had grown up on the same street in Buffalo, New York, and were quite old at the time, Mama being thirty-one and Papa twenty-nine. He was a master cooper by then, too, so he could bring her out west and support her right away.

Alas, I know that by the time I have a profession and a place in the world, Cécile will already be married to a Count or a Duke, and have two or three children. In the summer she'll live in a *château*, which is a big house in the country with a high wall, fountains, goldfish pools, and such, and in the winter she'll live in a grand apartment in the middle of Paris.

Taking the long-range view, however, and knowing that in this world of joy and woe anything can happen, I believe there may be hope for me. Her husband could be much older, and die of old age, or if he's not so old, he could die in battle or in a duel, leaving her a widow. If that happened, I would rush to her with gifts for her children. We would walk in her garden, and I would give her advice about the funeral and the best kind of monument to build, and I would stay by her side as long as she wanted me.

All sorts of people would crowd her grand house, but I would be the one she knew the best and trusted the most, because we had gone through storm and riot and triumph together, as you, Dear Reader, will see.

# I SEE CÉCILE GELINEAU FOR THE FIRST TIME, AND LEAVE FOR NEW ORLEANS

I started down the river the day I got back from the farm. The boat was called the *Lloyd Morris*. It was a rear-paddler, like the one Clayton and I had taken up the Missouri. It was due to leave at six-thirty at night, so it could get to the middle of the river and away from Saint Louis boat traffic when it was still daylight. The Captain was Mr. Robert Simon, a hard man. His great boast was that, no matter what might happen on the way, he always got his passengers to port on time.

Except for the wheelhouse on the roof, a riverboat is just a hotel set on a barge. The *Lloyd Morris* was a grander hotel than most. The top storey had twelve big bedrooms, a dining room with linen tablecloths and green glass flower vases, a sitting room, and a three-room apartment in front in case the owners wanted to go for a ride.

The next storey down had sixteen small cabins, plus a dining room and a big gambling saloon. The storey below that was all bedrooms. All three storeys had covered galleries going all the way around, so you could take a walk, or sit in a chair and read a book, or lean on the rail and watch the shore go by, and not get wet even if it was raining.

Deck level, where I was, we had a kitchen in front where they sold food and drink from six in the morning until ten at night. Back of that were storage rooms, an engine room with a big firewood bin, more storage rooms, and then four big rooms, two for men and two for women and children, with tables and benches for eating, and little closets with beds in them. They were steamy and smelly. Going to bed at night was like crawling into a tarpaper shack in July.

At the open ends of the boat there was space for wagons and crated-up cargo too big to be stored under cover. Children played hide-and-seek and Indian War there all day. That deck was so close to the water you could lean over and wash your hands.

When I got back to Saint Louis after visiting Mama and Papa, Mrs. Henze fed me an early dinner, and then she and Mr. Henze and their two little girls, Sophie and Susanne, brought me to the dock and came on board so the girls would have a chance to see what it was like being on a big riverboat. Mrs. Henze gave me a goody sack so I wouldn't have to buy food until the next night, and Mr. Henze, who was the most generous man in the world, gave me a pocket watch with a brass chain and key. I still have it, and it keeps good time.

When the whistle blew at six, such a crowd of people started coming up the gangway that the Henzes had to push to get off. Four people in that crowd I knew. The first was Mr. Nowac, a Canada Indian I knew from the trip up the Missouri. After the boiler on that boat exploded, he had gone down into the storeroom with me and held a lantern while I swam around among the shelves looking for a trunk I needed to find.

I had seen Indians in city suits before, but nobody like Mr. Nowac. He looked like a banker or a seminary teacher. He carried in his inside pocket a little book of French essays by Pascal, the famous French Thinker, and he would quote them sometimes. I don't know why it is, but white people who hate Indians hate educated ones the most. I called to him, but there was a lot of noise and he didn't hear me.

Right behind him came Mr. and Mrs. Rake and their little girl, Emily, who was asleep on Mrs. Rake's shoulder. I had met them just the week before, when we looked after the burial of their little boy, Seth, who had been carried off by the cholera and needed to be put in the ground in twenty-four hours. As every undertaker in the world will tell you, nothing is as hard as the death of a child. Emily was wearing the shoes we had taken off Seth's feet the last thing before closing the coffin, and they were bouncing against her mother's side.

Mr. Rake was right behind her, carrying a suitcase in each hand. He was somewhat drunk. He tripped halfway up and lost his grip on one of the suitcases. It would have fallen into the water, but the man behind him grabbed it and held it until he got his balance again. When the man offered to carry it the rest of the way up, Mr. Rake pulled it out of his hand and yelled curses at him. Mrs. Rake didn't even turn around. She just put her hand over Emily's free ear and kept walking.

On the dock, Susanne and Sophie were starting to fidget, so I took out an invisible pole and pretended I was fishing. It was a big mistake. The girls decided they were fish and started running around, weaving in and out through the crowd. Mrs. Henze ran after them and caught them, worried they were going to fall into the water, and Mr. Henze called out to me that it was time they left.

While we were waving goodbye, a jitney from the Star Hotel drove onto the dock. The last two people out of it were Cécile Gelineau and her brother, Dr. Alexandre Gelineau. Of course I didn't know who they were, or why they were traveling, but from the way he helped her down and talked to her walking toward the boat, I could see he was either her husband or a close relative.

He had a black band around his left arm, and she had on a black silk dress and bonnet. Clayton told me once that the Angels in Heaven grow black wings every Good Friday, and stand on clouds the whole day through singing hymns in honor of Jesus hanging on the cross. An organ with ebony pipes plays, the hymns sound like a Harmonic Hurricane, and the Angel Chorus looks like a forest at night with the moon shining down on it.

Imagine the most beautiful one of those Angels, and you will know what Cécile looked like.

The river was high and running fast, and the Captain had to keep the paddlewheel turning backward to take some of the strain off the ropes, which were as big around as a man's arm. The dock-gang boss, an old slave with white hair, stood next to the pier post at the back end working a long crowbar under the rope to help it slide in case the paddlewheel didn't give it enough slack when the time came to get loose from the dock.

Captain Simon blew the steam whistle and came running down to the first deck and along the gallery to the back of the boat. I could hear his shoes over my head. He stood in the spray from the paddlewheel and started yelling at the old slave. "I'll tell you when you need a crowbar. Get it out of there before I use this here iron rod on your head and drop your useless black body in the river."

He must have been carrying a rod with him, or picked one up that was loose, because he threw it at the man. It hit him on the shoulder and went banging and spinning across the dock. Most masters, when they hit a slave, want to see him flinch and hear him beg. Some even want him to try to run away and hide, as long as he doesn't cross the property line. Making a slave shake makes the master think he's better and smarter and stronger, all three. Captain Simon was that kind.

The slave didn't even look at his bleeding shoulder. He just stepped back from the post, pulling the crowbar out from under the rope, and stood there holding it and waiting.

The line of passengers on the gangway had stopped to watch.

Cécile was looking at the old slave with her eyes wide open and her hand at her mouth. I wanted to run down the gangplank and take her arm and lead her past all the other people on the gangway so she wouldn't have to see, but of course it was too late.

The Captain had nothing else to throw, and he was in a

hurry, so he stomped back up to the wheelhouse, cursing all the while. The gangway was clear now, and the deckhands started pulling it in. He ordered the paddle to turn faster and the ropes brought in. The front of the boat turned toward the dock, making that rope easy to get loose. The back one stayed tight and needed the crowbar. The old slave went and popped it like a cork out of a bottle, and then stood there with the crowbar in his hands.

We turned out into the river. The first part of my trip to France was starting.

## XII

I LEARN THAT EASY TRAVELING DEPENDS
ON MONEY, AND I VISIT WITH MR. NOWAC

Traveling is easier when you're rich. A top-deck ticket on the *Lloyd Morris* gets you a big room with pictures on the walls, lamps, chairs, and a four-foot-wide bed with sheets and blankets. You eat in a dining room with windows on two sides, you have your pick of everything on the menu, and there's no limit on seconds. When you need to write a letter, there's a parlor in the back with desks and lamps and free pens and paper. A waiter will fetch you a cup of coffee, or give you a deck of cards out of his coat pocket, just for the asking.

A bottom-deck ticket gets you a bunk in a sleeping closet for the entire trip, with space underneath for your valise. Almost everything else is extra. A blanket rents for twenty-five cents, and the same for a pillow. An envelope with two pieces of paper folded inside is a penny. I had my own envelopes and paper, and I didn't write any letters, anyway, until I was on the other ship, the one crossing the Atlantic Ocean. Stew from the kitchen at the back end is ten cents for a big bowl, five for refills. It's good. The first and second days they had slices of pie for a nickel. There's a place to wash, but you have to rent soap and a towel. Water for drinking is free, and they empty the barrels and fill them fresh every morning.

We were already out of sight of Saint Louis when the blanket and pillow room opened. After I found out the prices, I went outside to read Act Five of *The Tempest*. I should have been reading my French Bible already, but *The Tempest* is about a shipwreck, and people going to a foreign country and deciding if they want to stay or not. By the time I got to the end, where everybody goes home happy, I was hungry. I fetched Mrs. Henze's goody bag and started toward the front of the boat. Going along, I saw Mr. Nowac coming down the stairs. I wasn't sure he would remember me, but I slowed down, and when he saw me he put out his hand.

"Mr. Desant," he said, "it is good to see you again."

"I feel that way, too, Sir."

"You do much traveling, I see."

"It's only my second boat trip," I said. "It's just that I meet you every time."

"Did your friend wear the wedding dress you rescued that night?"

"Yes, thank you. It had some purple splotches from the wrapping paper, but it looked fine once we got it dry."

"You are traveling with?"

"I'm going to Paris by myself. Clayton went there last year."

"Desant is a French name."

"I guess so, but he's American from top to toe. I want to get him to come back home, where he'll be safe. What are you doing?"

"Transporting furs. Do you know minks?"

"I've heard of them, but I've never seen one."

"Small animals, very quick. I am on my way now to make certain the pelts have been stored high and dry. I will show you one, if you wish."

I followed him along to Storeroom One. You didn't need a key to get in the storerooms, but all the bins had padlocks. Mr. Nowac's bin was right next to the door. He took a key and opened it. Inside were four big parcels wrapped in oilcloth and tied with straps. On top of the top one was a leather pouch. He opened the pouch and took out a pelt and carried it outside and held it under a lantern.

"This is his coat for the Canada winter. It overcomes ice and snow and cold winds." He spread the paws apart so I could see the skin in between. "They swim, so they have webs, like ducks. Of course, not so wide. Minks are few and far between. They are difficult to trap. These parcels are from two seasons' trapping. It was a poor market in France last year, with the Revolution. It is better, now. I deliver them to New Orleans. At a trading firm. LaMaire. They send them to Paris, where a workshop sews them into coats for ladies."

We went back inside, and he locked everything up again. "Your brother may not want to come home from that Great City," he said.

"I hope he will. Would you like some sandwiches? They're

here in my goody bag, and I think there's some cake and dried plums and whatnot. The lady who packed it always puts in twice as much as you can eat."

"Yes, thank you."

We went to the front of the boat, and I sat with my back to the rail so I could watch the First Class gallery. Sparks were flying out of the smokestacks and twisting up into the sky, like silent fireworks. There were clouds over the moon, so you could see it was fixing to rain.

We didn't talk much. About eleven, Mr. Nowac left and went back up to his room on the second deck, but I stayed where I was. Near midnight there were noises of men having a fight in front of the gambling saloon. It didn't last long. Deckhands broke it up. I hoped my Angel was fast asleep and not hearing it.

I watched the river for a while, all black and silver. Right next to the boat the water seemed to be rushing along, but the trees on the shore were only creeping. It started to rain, and I decided to go to bed. On my way to the back of the boat a fat man came stumbling down the stairs from the second deck. He was slapping his hand against his white shirt, as if there were bugs there, and cursing under his breath. He almost knocked me down.

I had a dream. I was on a big riverboat getting ready to marry Clemmy, so that Clayton wouldn't have to. He hadn't asked me to do it, but I knew he wanted me to, and I knew I owed it to him. Being the groom, I had to go up and down from deck to deck making sure everybody knew how to find the Chapel. Mr. Henze walked next to me, carrying my black suit over his arm. Every time I stopped to put it on, something else would come up that I had to do instead.

I kept passing the room where Clemmy was. It was a big room full of mirrors and pianos. A gaggle of other girls was in with her, helping her climb into her white dress. Once, going past, I saw her half in and half out of it, with her hands pushing out through the arm holes. Then her head popped out with her hair piled up on top of it, but she was looking the other way, so she didn't see me.

At the end of the dream we couldn't find Clayton anywhere. Mr. Henze volunteered to take his place as Best Man. We were standing at the altar, waiting for Clemmy to come down the aisle. Her sister, Caroline, was playing the grand piano and smiling at me, trying to encourage me. I was standing behind a chair because I still hadn't had time to put my pants on. I was embarrassed, but I was glad, too, because I thought that when Clemmy saw me with no pants, she might get mad and not marry me.

## XIII

## I DISCOVER A DEAD MAN

When I woke up the next morning and it came to me that I wasn't going to have to marry Clemmy, I decided to stay awake. I pulled on my clothes and went outside. The deck was still wet from the rain, and there were puddles in the cargo covers, but the storm was over. A layer of mist was on the river, but I could see trees along the shore.

I walked to Storeroom One to make sure Mr. Nowac's minks were still dry and locked up. Then I went up two decks to the gambling saloon, thinking there might be a basket of bread, or a dish of pickles, or something else left over from the night. A man was asleep on a sofa on the far side of the saloon. On the table next to him was a basket of Dutch braided rolls and a dish of mustard. I went over and took a roll and dipped both ends, and then walked out the open door on that side and went to the front of the boat and stood there watching the river and eating my roll. Hard as it was, it was good.

On the left, the sun had turned the mist as red as water-melon. It sparkled like watermelon, too. Over the splash of the water and the rumble of the steam engine, I could hear the birds calling to each other in the trees. A big heron flew slowly across toward the west shore, as if his wings were oars and he was a boat, and landed in the mud. As soon as he was finished folding his wings he caught a frog, threw it in the air, and swallowed it. It made a lump going down his neck.

After a while I looked down to the rail where Mr. Nowac and I had been sitting and eating, and saw a dead man lying on his side. It was the fat man I had seen swatting his chest on my way to bed. His white shirt was wet, and stuck to his body, and his face was as gray as wash water. A dead man can look asleep, but it's a stiller sleep than a living man ever has.

Though I knew in my heart there was no help for him, I ran down there to make sure. He had hit his head when he fell, and bled a little onto the deck. The rain had thinned the blood out and spread it around. I put my hand under his shirt to feel his chest. It was cold and rubbery. Then I ran up to the wheelhouse. There were three men there, Captain Simon sitting on a chair with a stumpy unlit cigar in his mouth, the Purser at a table in the corner writing in a ledger, and the Steersman standing at the wheel.

Captain Simon tilted his head back and looked at me over his cigar. "What are you doing here?"

"Excuse me, Sir, but there's a dead man on the bottom deck, in the front of the boat."

He sucked at the cigar stump, as if he thought it might still be lit, and then he took it out of his mouth and looked at it carefully. "You must not have heard me, boy. I said you got no business here."

"There's a dead man on the bottom deck," I said again. "I went down and looked at him close up to be sure."

He pointed at a sign over the door: *No Admittance*. "See that? You able to read?"

I stepped back out the door and stood on the walkway. "I'm sorry," I said, "but there really is a dead man. I thought you'd want to know."

"Why you standing out there? You going away?"

"No, Sir."

"Well, don't." He reached in his pocket and took out a match, lit it, and put it under his cigar. The two last fingers on his right hand were missing. He kept puffing away until there was blue smoke all around him. "My timetable is my religion," he said. "Dying on this ship ain't something I allow."

He got up from his chair and called to the First Mate, who was on the walkway on the other side. "I'm going to take this boy down to the cargo deck and pitch him in the river," he said. "It won't take me long."

He led the way down the stairs, but instead of going all the way to the bottom deck he went along the First Class gallery and leaned over the front rail. "Point it out," he said.

The mist had pretty much burned off the river, and the sun was brighter, so the shadows were darker. "He's there next to the pine crate with the pipe sticking out the side."

"Don't see nothing."

"He's really down there."

"I see him. He's a drunk," he said.

"It could look that way from here, but I went down and felt him. He's been dead half the night."

"Kick him hard, he'll wake up."

"You could kick him all day," I said.

"Don't sass me, boy." He made a little fist with his three-fingered hand and rubbed it back and forth on the rail. I remembered how he had thrown that iron rod at the old slave the day and I thought he might be fixing to hit me.

"If we go there, he's dead, Sir. I'm in undertaking, so I know dead wh Lying outdoors, he's bound to draw a crowd. They alw.

Just then, like a character walking out onto the stage in a play, a man came around the corner and went to the body and leaned over it, studying it.

Captain Simon yelled at him. "Hey, Mister! What you doing? Looking down a well? Stop your fool gawking! Get along!"

The man looked up and shrugged his shoulders, but he didn't move.

The Captain threw away his cigar and led me back up to the wheelhouse. The Purser, Mr. Harris, was still behind the desk in the corner with his book.

"We got a doctor in First Class. What's his name?"

Mr. Harris turned back two pages and ran his finger down the edge. "Gelineau," he said.

"Bring him to the bottom deck at the prow end. And pull out one of those Death Certificates from the top right drawer and give it to me, just in case this boy isn't a complete fool."

Mr. Harris took out a little piece of paper and wrote down Dr. Gelineau's room number, unlocked a tin box and pulled out a paper, gave it to Captain Simon, and left.

The Captain slowly folded the certificate and put it in his pocket. Then, to show that nobody could make him hurry, he went to the front window and stood there. There was a bend about a quarter of a mile ahead, and he tilted his head as if he was calculating how far it was in feet and inches. After a while he turned around and looked at the First Mate. "Cheat to starboard as we go around. That opposite bank's shallower than the chart says."

Then we went down to where the body was. A deckhand was standing guard. The man who had come along first was standing next to him, and there was a crowd, men and women both. The Captain laid his foot on the dead man's shoulder and rolled him onto his back.

I heard a little girl say, "He's dead, ain't he, Ma?" It was Emily Rake. She had gotten away from her mother and slid between people's legs and was standing at the front of the crowd. Emily looked at me and waved, but her eyes went right back to the body. "Look, Mama, blood," she said.

A sight like that can give a child bad dreams, so I spit on

my handkerchief and bent down and wiped the blood off the man's face. He had fallen so hard he had broken off one of his front teeth, and it was buried inside his lower lip. I pulled it out and balled it up in my handkerchief.

"Throw it overboard," Captain Simon said.

I started to put it in my pocket and he hit my hand hard enough for the tooth and hankie together to fly into the water. Emily ran over to the rail to see where it hit.

The boat was going around the bend now. The near bank was full of lilac bushes. I went over and picked Emily up and told her to take a deep breath. "Smell it," I said. "It's just like perfume."

She pointed to my handkerchief, which was floating flat on the river, like a piece of paper.

"The current's carrying it right along," I said. "Maybe it'll beat us to New Orleans."

Then Mrs. Rake came and took Emily from me and carried her away.

The Captain went down on his knees next to the man and began searching through his pockets. "You're too young to be an undertaker," he said. "You just want what you can steal from him."

That made me mad. "I worked for Henze's Funeral Parlor in Saint Louis," I said. "I've got a character from Mr. Henze if you want to see it."

He pulled a wallet out of the man's pants pocket and stood up and opened it. The flap had a name burned into it: Samuel Brevoort. The Captain took the money out. "He owes me extra for the trouble he's putting me through. Then there's the coffin, carrying and depositing costs, and dock fees. Paperwork don't come cheap, either."

By now there were more people standing around. "What's holding Harris up?" the Captain asked. "Where's the Doctor? Everybody keep back until the Doctor comes."

## XIV

## I MEET DR. GELINEAU

After a minute, Dr. Gelineau came through the crowd, carrying a little leather bag. He was taller than he had looked coming up the gangplank. His hair was gray. I found out later that most of the people in the Gelineau family go gray by the time they're thirty.

He knelt down on the deck, unsnapped his bag, took out a mirror, put it in front of Mr. Brevoort's mouth, and watched to see if it clouded up. It didn't. Then he took a wooden stick shaped like a trumpet, but shorter, laid the wide end on Mr. Brevoort's chest, put his ear to the narrow end, and listened for a heartbeat. After that he pushed back the man's eyelids, looked in each eye, and closed them again. Then he stood up and bowed to Captain Simon. "Dr. Alexandre Gelineau, at your service. This man is beyond human help."

Captain Simon put Mr. Brevoort's wallet in his pocket and they shook hands. "I knew that," the Captain said. "I can spot a dead man a mile away. Frenchie, right?" He took the Death Certificate out of his shirt and unfolded it. "Fill out this here certificate, sign it at the bottom, put the date in, and that's all I need out of you. Five minutes. Less. And there'll be a fee for your services. I don't expect a man to do anything out of charity."

Dr. Gelineau shook his head. "I teach medicine, so I have a professional interest in what causes a man to die. No fee will be required."

"I never owe anybody a penny or a favor," Captain Simon said. "One way or another, I'll see you're paid. Money's always best, but if money ain't your taste, I'll find something else. This here boy will be your assistant, strip him down, wash him for you, help box him up when you're done. He's young, but he's had years in the business. He'll do it trim or answer to me."

Dr. Gelineau turned to me and put out his hand. "Alexandre Gelineau. You are?"

"Henry Desant."

Captain Simon held up Mr. Brevoort's wallet, pulled out his ticket and waved it in the air. "This says *Destination: Cape Girardeau*, and Cape Girardeau's where we're leaving him. That's under three hours." He looked at the deckhand standing guard. "You're in charge of this piece of flotsam, Bill. Get three men to help haul him into the wood bin. I don't want the Doctor here sending me a bill for fixing ruptures. Roll him up in a tarp."

Bill left to get the other men.

Captain Simon poked Mr. Brevoort in the belly with his foot. "Nine drunks out of ten are big as whales. You ever notice that, Doctor? Why is it? Ain't no fat in whiskey, and a man like this drinks all his meals, so how come he's all blubber? By the way, I should warn you, that wood bin's by the steam engine, so it's hot in there. No matter. You'll be in and out directly, so you won't have time to notice. Winter or summer, flesh don't keep as good on the river as it does on dry land. Now why you suppose that is?"

"I must request, Captain," Dr. Gelineau said, "a cool place with good light."

"You're just making extra work for yourself. My advice, keep your hands clean. Do your job right here on the spot. You got sunlight, a nice breeze. Take one look at his nose, you know what killed him, a hide full of liquor. He came down here to use the deck for a privy, fell, and split his head open. Nothing a drunk does better or easier."

"You are probably correct," Dr. Gelineau said.

"You don't want to insult the poor sack of lard? Write down 'old age.' Close enough. Nobody, not the Sheriff or nobody else, wants to know the true reason. Words on paper. Just make sure you don't write down it was a contagious disease. Do that and we'll all be in quarantine in New Orleans Harbor for thirty days, slapping chiggers and eating gumbo for breakfast, lunch, and dinner."

"I did see him drunk last night," I said.

Captain Simon spread his hands. "Eyewitness testimony. Gospel truth out of the mouths of babes. We can go up the steps to the First Class Dining Room right this minute, and you can write it out over a glass. Not a bad morning's work."

Dr. Gelineau shook his head. "Sir, having been called in to the case, I must make an examination. There is no other way.

If I can be provided with a high table along with a cool room on the sun side, the work may go faster."

The Captain shrugged his shoulders. "Doctor's orders is Holy Writ here. Lucky for you, you got this experienced undertaker to move everything along. A dollar for your work, boy, as soon as we're out of Cape Girardeau."

"I don't want pay, either," I said.

"See your influence, Doctor? The Mississippi is a river of miracles." He made a fist, looked at it, and punched me in the arm. "You do a good job, you'll get paid, boy, no matter what you say."

The men brought the tarp through the crowd. "Carry him to Storeroom Three, starboard side," the Captain said. "It's cooler and not so noisy. Find a high table for the Doctor. And put an oilcloth under it so the floor don't get stained."

The four men spread out the tarp next to Mr. Brevoort, rolled him up like a cigarette, and carried him through the crowd to the storeroom.

"I got a first-class doctoring kit in my locker you can use," the Captain said. "Every tool from a little bitty tweezer all the way up to a bone saw fit to take the leg off an elephant."

Dr. Gelineau took a key out of his pocket. "Thank you very much, but I have my instruments enough at hand."

"Better and better. One other thing. Once you done your job, not before, mind you, take a look at that cut on the poor fellow's head. We got a savage down from Canada on this boat. I don't sell the tickets, or he wouldn't be here. My theory is, he come upon this poor fellow after he was dead and tried to lift his scalp. A *souvenir*, as you French say."

"He'd never do that," I said. "I know him."

Captain Simon smiled at me. "Is that where you learned the undertaking trade, among the savages? They'll give you all the business you want, that's for sure."

I didn't say anything back.

"We will need a large basin of hot water, and a second basin, and some clean rags," Dr. Gelineau said, and then he looked at me. "And, in addition?"

"His Sunday suit, if he has one."

"Yes, excellent. Look into Mr. Brevoort's luggage and see if he has a clean suit in which we could dress him. And perhaps you could have someone bring us a pot of strong coffee."

"No other kind we got. And here's what I've decided. When you're done, I'm going to move you into the apartment on the top deck. Belongs to the owners, but they ain't here, and the place is mine to dispose of as I will. Runs all the way across the front, windows from end to end, no finer accommodations on the Nile and neither the Amazon. It's yours as soon as you write down on this here certificate that the man died natural."

Dr. Gelineau picked up his doctor kit. "Follow Mr. Brevoort's body," he said to me. "I must tell my sister my business, and get my larger bag. I won't be five minutes."

## XV

## DR. GELINEAU GIVES
## ME AN ANATOMY LESSON

Death is always sad and lonely, even when the dead man is a drunk nobody knows. That's why, back in Saint Louis, whenever I was doing up a body alone, I would always try to make it a social occasion. I would talk to the dead man about different Shakespeare characters, or ask him how he came by one of his scars, or tell him what kind of weather we could expect at the cemetery when the time came. If I ran out of things to talk about and there was still work to do, I would sing hymns.

The one thing I would never talk about to a dead man was what I was going to do when I was finished working on him. That would have been like saying, "I'm alive and you're dead. Ha ha ha."

When Dr. Gelineau came into the storeroom with his kit, I had Mr. Brevoort scrubbed down and I was drying his feet and telling him about the drunk sailors in *The Tempest*. I didn't know the Doctor was behind me until he came around and put his kit on the floor.

"I also talk in the presence of the dead," he said. "Most often I'm giving a lecture to my students, but when I am alone with the poor creature, I sometimes lecture him."

He took a tray out of the lid and set it on the table next to Mr. Brevoort's head, picked out a scalpel, and felt around on the bare chest for the best spot to begin. When he found it, he laid his finger there to mark the place.

"You do not expect to become faint?"

"I've never helped a doctor before, but I'm wide awake and fine as long as I have work to do."

"That is the trick, certainly. A post-mortem is a thousand times easier when you have duties." He put his scalpel next to his finger and pushed the point down into Mr. Brevoort's chest. "So, we set out to discover why this man lost his life, doing as little damage as possible."

Just then a steward brought coffee, and another one brought Mr. Brevoort's suit and a clean shirt. They put them on a crate just inside the door. After that came two men with a pine coffin, which they left outside the door.

Dr. Gelineau made a deep cut across Mr. Brevoort's chest and drew the flesh back from the ribs on the left side. The quick way he did it made me think of Papa, who can cut the Christmas goose apart into twelve portions in eleven strokes.

He asked me to take a pair of heavy scissors out of his kit, and to snip two ribs at the breastbone. I told him about Papa and the goose, and then I asked him a question. "Mama says there's a Spark of Life that comes into you when you're born and goes out of you when you die," I said. "Is that what you think?"

He waited until I was through with the scissors, and then he asked for a pair of copper posts to keep the ribs apart. "If your mother says it's true, it must be. She is a woman, so she knows better. I only know we are part of a chain. Now, hold that mirror and reflect some light into his chest. In your right hand, please. Good. Lean your hip against his hip, and put your left hand on his right shoulder." He probed around for a minute. "Here's our quarry. The heart."

I asked him the word for it in French.

"*Le coeur*," he said. "A machine with many parts. Each part has its own Latin name, so that doctors in London and Paris and Saint Petersburg and Cairo can discuss their observations and treatments without misunderstanding one another. It is the same principle as the one held by the Catholic Church. Wherever in the world a Catholic man finds himself on Sunday, he can enter a Catholic church and hear the same Latin words he has heard since childhood. He may not understand them, but he is glad at the familiar sounds. Each part of the heart has a French name as well, but you will have to ask a butcher if you wish to know what they are."

"Latin is fine," I said.

"Give me that knife with the hook at the end. I found it in Mexico. Now, back to your post with the mirror." He cut some connections and lifted Mr. Brevoort's heart halfway out of his chest, cut the fat from the top of it, and examined it for a long time, turning it this way and that. Finally, he held a corner of it up for me to see.

"The Captain was right. This man drank and ate himself to death. The heart tried to assist him by growing larger, but that only made it worse and worse. He insulted it again and again until last night. Then a clot of blood made a barricade across this vessel, and the lion's share of his blood was dammed up."

He cut out about six inches of artery and took it to the door and looked at it in sunlight. He asked me to take his glasses off and clean them and put them back on him.

"See, the man was fighting against himself, and here is the barricade that caused his death. Feel it. Hard, yes? Like barely cooked macaroni."

I felt it.

Then he went back to the table, cut a piece of artery out of Mr. Brevoort's neck, and carried it to the door. That was when I learned my second French word, *cou*, which means "neck." Even today, if I say that word, I see Mr. Brevoort's body lying on the table. After that, Dr. Gelineau decided to look at his liver, which meant another cut, but first we had some coffee. The liver looked just the way he expected it to. He put it back inside and stitched the wounds up, and I dipped up fresh river water in a bucket and gave him a last wash. When we had dried him off, I took a look at his forehead, just above his nose. "Nobody tried to take his scalp off, did he?"

"No. It is a ridiculous idea."

The deckhands, who had been waiting outside, took the lid off the coffin. They didn't want to bother dressing him, but Dr. Gelineau said we had to. They made a joke of it, but we got him looking presentable.

## XVI

## CAPTAIN SIMON TREATS
## MR. NOWAC SPITEFULLY

As we were going up to the wheelhouse to tell the Captain we were done, I told Dr. Gelineau about Mr. Nowac, mostly because he was a French-speaking Indian. When we walked into the wheelhouse, Mr. Nowac was there, standing by the Purser's desk with the Captain in front of him. The Captain kept his eyes on him, but talked to Dr. Gelineau.

"This here savage has crept in among us with the aim of committing criminal acts upon our persons."

"That's not so," I said.

Captain Simon turned and pointed at me with his cigar. "You'll keep your mouth shut, boy, if you expect to be paid, and even if you don't."

"Mr. Nowac is an old friend of mine," Dr. Gelineau said. "He runs a respectable fur trapping business."

The Captain shook his head. "You never saw him before in your life. He's a stranger to you. You cut people open and examine their guts, Doctor, but God alone sees the heart.

Lookee how this man's face slopes. He'd scalp every man, woman, and child of us if he could. They all want to do it, deep down in their hearts."

He turned back to Mr. Nowac. "My advice to you, my red friend, is to get the best price you can for your cargo, as fast as you can, and get off my boat."

The Captain took the death certificate out of his pocket and put it on the Purser's desk. "But, first things first. I was right about our dead friend, wasn't I? Drink did him in."

Dr. Gelineau nodded his head. "With the aid of gluttony."

"So you didn't have to get your hands dirty on him. It was your choice. Get up from your chair, Mr. Harris, and give the Doctor room to write. Use the pen that's there, Sir. If you need help, just ask." He pushed the Steersman aside and looked out the front window at the river as if nobody else was in the room.

Dr. Gelineau went to the desk and sat down and read the certificate from top to bottom. Then he took the pen and wrote. When he was done, he signed it.

The Captain gave the wheel back to the Steersman, read the certificate over, taking a long time, and then he folded it up and put it in his pocket.

"You did your duty, Doctor. Well, I know how to do mine. I already moved you and your sister into the Owners' Apartment. You'll find her there now, drinking tea or coffee, her choice. Ten windows heading south, three generous rooms, including parlor."

"A *fait accompli*," Dr. Gelineau said.

"Meaning what, in plain English?"

"Something already done, so there is no point refusing."

"You'll thank me when you see it."

"You went to unnecessary trouble," Dr. Gelineau said. "But I do thank you. Now, if we are done?"

"Almost done, almost done. I have to pay your assistant. Fair's fair, and generous is generous. I don't look down on paymaster's work." He took a silver dollar out of his coat pocket and pushed it into my fist. I wanted to refuse it, but I wasn't brave enough.

"One more thing for you, Dr. Gelineau. A medical question. Say you see a body floating in the river, and you fish it out and cut it up and spread the organs out on a table. Can you tell from what's in front of you if it's a White Man? Even if he's turned black outside and bloated from a month in the warm Mississippi, there must be signs."

"If you opened him up, you would see what you wanted to see," Dr. Gelineau said.

Captain Simon smiled and shook his head. "You're trying to provoke me, Doctor, but you can't. Not now, when I've had my way. I'm asking you a simple question, one White Man to another, and I'm looking for a simple answer. Say a slave gets himself killed and dropped into the water, or drowns trying to escape his rightful owner. It might be he's a strong young buck with a reward on his head, dead or alive. On the other hand, it might be he's a White Man deserving of Christian burial. He couldn't help turning black. The question is, if I sliced him open, what's in his liver, let's say, to tell me his original color?"

"Nothing," Dr. Gelineau said.

The Captain looked at Mr. Nowac. "Just because the Doctor pretends to be your friend and won't tell me the signs, it don't mean I ain't the Captain of this boat or that I wouldn't slice a man open just out of curiosity, if I took a mind to."

Dr. Gelineau and I went out the door, but the Captain followed us out onto the walkway. "You want to think the worst of me, Doctor. Suit yourself. That's your privilege. I thank you for your services. Now I give you my permission to go. And don't try to make life safe for that savage. I decide everything that happens on this boat, both big and small."

## XVII

## I MEET CÉCILE

Cécile opened the Owner's Apartment door as soon as Dr. Gelineau knocked. He introduced us, and she gave me her hand. It was cool, and her fingers were long and smooth. She was wearing a black dress without any frills, and she had a black ribbon holding her hair back. Her eyes were gray, with flecks of copper. They made me think of rain clouds when the sun starts coming through.

We went in. There were sofas and chairs everywhere, a table with food on it next to one of the windows, an ebony-wood cabinet full of china dishes and geegaws, and small tables with lamps on them with colored glass shades. It was the biggest parlor I had ever been in, with the most windows. The sun was making diamonds on the carpet.

Cécile brought me over to the table. "Certainly, after a morning of work, you must have a second breakfast," she said. There were two kinds of bread, plus boiled eggs and butter and jam and coffee and tea.

"I saw you yesterday, Mr. Desant," she said while she was pouring me coffee. "We were in the jitney crossing the dock, and we passed two little girls waving to you, and you were waving to them in return."

"They're the children of my old boss," I said.

"How good of them to come, and how happy for you. Will you travel all the way to New Orleans?"

"Yes. Then to Paris."

"Oh? On what ship, if I may ask?"

"I don't know. The first one that'll sell me a ticket."

"The Atlantic is quiet at this season, Dr. Gelineau tells me. In the month of September, when we were last at sea, there were some few storms."

Dr. Gelineau told her in English how Captain Simon had been with Mr. Nowac. I was sorry, because it made her unhappy.

We kept talking and eating for almost an hour. Then the sun on the carpet began to swing around fast, showing we were turning into Cape Girardeau. We got up and went out onto the front gallery to watch. I asked Cécile, calling her Miss Gelineau, of course, if she wanted me to fetch her parasol.

"Thank you, no, Mr. Desant. Dr. Gelineau informs me that some little sun adds health," she said.

We were running crosswise to the current, coming into the dock from the upriver side. Mr. Brevoort's coffin was next to the drawn-up gangway, waiting to be unloaded. We hit the dock hard, and Cécile had to grab onto a post to steady herself. She wasn't wearing any rings, and she had a little freckle in the shape of a heart on the back of her left hand.

The crew put out only one rope, but the current held us fast to the dock. Captain Simon ran off as soon as the gangway was let down, and went to the Dockmaster's shack. There was a boy standing in front of it, and the Captain gave him some money and sent him running to get the Sheriff. Then he went inside. After a minute he came out and waved, and four deckhands carried the coffin off the boat and over to the far side of the shack, in the shade.

After five minutes the boy came back, and right behind him the Sheriff, and a preacher in a black frock coat. The Dockmaster gave the Sheriff the death certificate, slid the coffin out into the sun, and pried up the lid a few inches to give the Sheriff a peek inside. They all three shook hands, the Captain came back, they pulled up the gangway and untied the rope, and we scraped out along the dock and back into the channel. I bid Dr. Gelineau and Cécile goodbye.

"May we make you an invitation to dine with us tonight?" Cécile said. "It will be a true American meal. They are serving beef and catfish, but not on the same plate. The Steward told me they will not catch the fish until after noon, and that they do not have the flavor of cats at all."

Because Papa and Mama always taught me to say no, thank you, to the first invitation to supper, and then accept the second one, I said no, thank you.

"How sad," she said. "Perhaps some other evening?"

"Yes, thank you," I said, and left. On the stairs to the bottom deck, I told myself it was right not to force my company on them. Cécile didn't know me at all, and she needed to be alone to talk French with her brother. Still, I felt that passing up the chance had been a big mistake.

## XVIII

## MR. NOWAC ASKS ME TO DO HIM A FAVOR

Mr. Nowac came down to the bottom deck after the one o'clock bell, and I asked him if I could help him.

"I will leave the boat," he said.

I didn't say anything because I thought he was smart to do it. We went to the back of the boat and got our plates of stew. He paid. They still had good-looking pie, but I wasn't that hungry. We sat down just past the line of paddlewheel spray. He waited to talk until our plates were almost clean.

"I will get off in Caruthersville early tomorrow morning. I will wait there for the boat *Timberland*, coming behind this boat in three days. I know a priest in the town. He will be happy for my company. You can assist by helping me to carry off my furs. Warning, however. The packets are heavy."

"They can't be that heavy. I'll do whatever you need. Will you lose money?"

"Not if you help me. I cannot stay. Every trader must value his cargo in dollars, and pay the freight, before it is loaded on the boat. Captain Simon offered me a third of my price, in cash. I said I would consider it, but I cannot. I will miss your company and this excellent horse-meat stew, but I will have a visit with my friend to compensate me."

"Is that what this is? Horse meat?"

"Well cooked."

I had never eaten horse meat before, at least that I knew. It tasted good, so I finished the last bits. We took our plates back to the kitchen and went forward to Storeroom One to look at the bin with his minks in it.

"If I do not get off," he said, "these will be taken in the night. If I then ask the Captain where they have gone, he will tell me I should have taken the price he offered."

"How much is that?"

"Seven hundred ten dollars. It is money in the hand, but I have signed a contract with the LaMaire Company. Moreover, I will not surrender my goods."

"I could help you guard them," I said. "We could go turn and turn about. It's only four more nights. The one on watch could sleep on the floor."

"No, thank you from my heart. My goods and I must go. I am lucky to have found out my danger before Caruthersville. My friend will take me in."

"The next boat could have a Captain as bad."

He pulled out his key to be sure he still had it. "Rousseau tells us that cruelty grows out of a man's fear of his own weakness, and this particular Captain fears very much. He would dance on my grave, if he had the chance."

I reached into my pocket, took out the dollar Captain Simon had paid me, went out of the storeroom, and threw it as far as I could into the river.

Mr. Nowac came after me. "You will not grow rich using your arm in that way."

"It was sweating blood in my pocket," I said. "What else can I do to help?"

I was half sorry the minute I said it, thinking he might tell me he wanted me to get off with him, which would mean not ever seeing Dr. Gelineau and Cécile again.

He took a sealed envelope out of his pocket, plus a sample pelt tied in oilcloth. On the envelope, written in big letters, was "LaMaire Company, Import and Export."

"I want you to give the letter and the pelt to Mr. LaMaire. Into his hand only, even if you must come back later in the day to find him. The letter tells him that I am three days delayed. His place of business is on the docks. A sign is over the building. You will have no trouble finding it."

I took the envelope and the pelt and put them inside my shirt and told him I would deliver them as soon as the boat got to New Orleans.

"After you give them to Mr. LaMaire, do not leave. Wait until he has read them both and dismissed you. Yes?"

"I'll wait until he tells me to go."

"Good. Thank you."

We were due in Caruthersville at dawn, so as soon as it got dark I sat down with Mr. Nowac by the storeroom door. Around midnight he told me I should go to bed, and he would come wake me, but I wasn't sure he would. We talked on and off. I told him I was going to Paris to save my brother, if I could. He thought it was too dangerous for a boy alone. I asked him to teach me the words for "thief" and "innocent," which are *voleur* and *innocent*.

We came into Caruthersville just as the sun was coming up. The packs of furs were heavy, as he had said, and I had to borrow a big-wheeled dolly for my two. There was a lot of cargo coming and going, and nobody paid any attention to us. We could have been thieves ourselves, and no one the wiser.

## XIX

## CÉCILE SITS BY ME IN THE NIGHT, AND I
## SEE A PICTURE OF HER DEAD BROTHER

It was my third day on the boat, and I still hadn't done any French study, so I opened my valise, took out the French Bible and the French-English dictionary, went outside, found a crate to lean up against, and began to read Psalm One Hundred. I knew the English by heart, so I didn't think I'd have to use the dictionary much, but as it turned out the only French words I was sure of were "age" and "joyful," *âge* and *joyeux* in French. Clayton says foreign words are like chiggers, but after I'd been looking back and forth between the Bible and the dictionary for a while, the French and English words both began to look like bugs of one sort or another. So I stopped and shut my eyes and fell asleep where I sat.

Dr. Gelineau woke me up and said I should go inside and sleep on my bed, but that was because he didn't know how hot those little sleeping closets were. He had come down looking for Mr. Nowac, and I told him he was safe with his goods. "You may have saved his life," he said. Then he asked me to have dinner with them that night, up on the top deck, and I said yes.

I didn't want to go empty-handed, so when the boat docked in Osceola around two o'clock, to unload some Saint Louis machinery, and I saw some pretty flowers on the riverbank, I went to gather a bouquet. There were three big clumps of different kinds, so it went fast. When the whistle blew I turned around to climb back up the bank and grabbed on to what I thought was a root but turned out to be a snake. He bit me on the back of my left hand, and then just held on. Clayton says there's one special devil whose only job is teaching serpents how to swim. If that's true, this serpent was in luck, because I shook him off into the water as I ran along the dock.

Mrs. Rake, who was standing on the deck, saw what I had been doing, found a bucket, dipped up some water for me to put the flowers in, and got some rags to bandage up my hand. Mama always says binding a bite does nothing but squeeze the polluted blood closer to your heart, so I said no, thank you. The bite hurt, but not much, and I just sat down by the rail and sucked out whatever poison I could and spit it overboard. The rest of the afternoon I kept my hand up in the air as much as I could. The great thing was that I had the flowers. It was a big bunch.

By dinnertime, my hand was swolt up and turning purple, but the color was only on the back of it, and it didn't hurt much. I had to ask Mrs. Rake to button my dress shirt and tie my necktie, and I had a little trouble getting my hand to go through the arm of my funeral suit, but that sleeve was a tight fit to start with. When I was done, I thought I could hold it under the table so they wouldn't notice.

Cécile was by the door and invited me inside. "My brother will appear in a moment," she said, putting the flowers into a green glass vase. She had on a black dress that made a rustling noise as she walked. It made me think of Mama, who always wore a noisy robe when Clayton and I were sick, so when we called for her in the night, we'd hear her coming before we saw her.

We went to dinner as soon as Dr. Gelineau came out of his room. Sitting in the First Class dining room was like sitting in a super-elegant downtown restaurant with a steam engine rumbling in the cellar. Dr. Gelineau and Cécile probably thought I was trying to be extra-polite, holding my left hand in my lap while we ate our soup and fish. The catfish meat fell off the bones with nothing but a fork. Unfortunately, the beef needed a knife, so they saw the purple. Dr. Gelineau told me we had to do something for it right away, so we all three went to their cabin. He sat me in a chair with my arm on a high table, and Cécile got a pair of fine scissors and cut along the seam of my jacket so I could get my arm out of it, and rolled my shirtsleeve up. After feeling my arm up and down, Dr. Gelineau took out his scalpel. "Never fear," he said. "It's been in brandy since we used it yesterday."

Some doctors can cut you so quick and clean, you don't know they've done it until you look. Dr. Gelineau is one of them. He made a cut across my arm two inches north of the bite, and it hardly hurt at all. After he got some blood out of it he sewed it up and laid a poultice on it, and Cécile put a bandage on it. I was ready to go back to dinner, but they told me I had to stay in their apartment and sleep on their sofa that night. "Miss Gelineau will sing you to sleep. It was for the sake of her attention that you invited the snake to bite you, was it not?"

This was the first I knew she sang, but I wasn't surprised. "I'm just sorry to be taking you away from your supper," I said.

"No need to apologize," Dr. Gelineau said. "It's good to give your belly a rest between fish and flesh. We are going to return and finish our supper immediately. And we'll stay for American pie."

As soon as they left I remembered the sample pelt Mr. Nowac had given me for an earnest at the LaMaire Company, which I had put in my valise, so I ran down to the bottom deck as fast as I could and got it out. There were lots of people everywhere on all the galleries, so nobody paid me any attention. I knew that Captain Simon would know that Mr. Nowac was gone, and want revenge on me for helping him, so I hung on to the rails with my good hand going down the steps and up both, and watched behind me. Running hard made my hand start bleeding a little bit, but not much. When I got back to their apartment I put the pelt under the sofa and lay back down. Five minutes later, Dr. Gelineau and Cécile walked in with a piece of pie for me.

While I was eating the pie, I told them about Clayton leaving Saint Louis and going to Paris to start a Chapel. It was hard to make Cécile understand what he had done.

"His Bishop must have great faith in him," she said.

"He doesn't have a bishop. He's his own church. The Angel Gabriel came to him in a dream and told him to go."

"Gabriel did not tell him to learn French first?"

"No."

"How many Frenchmen did he expect would sit under him?"

"He's got fifteen, and a Deacon to translate for him. The trouble is, the Deacon's a thief, and so are all the rest. Clayton doesn't know it. I'm going to tell him. I hope he believes me."

"He will, once you open his eyes."

"I'm not so sure."

"Not believe his own brother?"

"He has strong ideas, and he thinks I do nothing but tell lies."

I didn't want to talk about it anymore, so I yawned and blinked, and they said good night and went to their rooms. In the middle of the night, I rolled over on my left hand and let out a yelp. Cécile came out of her room right away and sat down next to me. She had put her hair in a long braid, and when she leaned over it came loose and dropped on my arm. Immediately, most of my pain went away. She undid the poultice and lifted it off and laid her fingers on the back of my hand to see how hot it was, and then she turned up the lamp to look at the color. The purple had spread a little, but it wasn't any darker.

"I'm sorry I woke you up," I said.

"I was awake, thinking about your brother among his

thieves. You must tell him discreetly, once, right away, and if he does not believe you, you must go."

"I'll be careful," I said.

"And you mustn't worry about this little wound. I do not know what you call it in English," she said. "In French, we call it a *cicatrice*. Look here." She stretched her right arm out under the light and put her finger on her wrist. "I received a long, long wound once, from a glass window, from here to where my arm bends. Dr. Gelineau sewed it together, and now there is only this little line. See?"

It was like a white thread with a curl at her elbow. "I don't mind," I said. "I got a much bigger scar in my leg from going over a wire fence when I was little."

She turned down the lamp. "I will stay until you are ready to sleep again. First some medicine for sleep, and then I shall sing you a song."

She went into her room and brought out a bottle of laudanum mixed with raspberry syrup and gave me a spoonful. Then she sang "London Bridge," and after that a French song. Next to the lamp, in a black frame, was a drawing of a boy in a military-school uniform. It had a black ribbon around it. Now I knew they were mourning their little brother.

## XX

## I PLAY CARDS WITH A SHARP

The next three days went by fast. Every day early in the morning, Dr. Gelineau would come down and look at my arm to see that it was fine. Then I would eat and go to the front of the boat and read in my French Bible for a while, and make lists of words. I'd do the same thing after lunch. I made friends with Emily Rake and taught her to say "sky," "mud," "moon," and "bird" in French. She sounded ten times more French than I did.

The day before we were due in New Orleans, Dr. Gelineau took the bandage off and gave me back the coat from my funeral suit. Cécile had stitched the seam in the sleeve back up so you couldn't see it had ever been undone. Then he invited me to eat dinner with them.

I got dressed half an hour ahead and went out on deck to watch the card playing. It was a rule on the boat that you couldn't play cards for money anywhere but the gambling room, and the Captain was strict about it, but that last day the deckhands were too busy getting the cargo ready to be unloaded to pay any attention, so there were poker games going on everywhere, with money right out in the open.

Mr. Rake was playing Blind Blackjack with a cardsharp named Frank Spellman. I was by the rail with Mrs. Rake and Emily, watching. I knew the game. It's not very interesting, and it depends too much on luck, but Mr. Henze and I used to play it from time to time just for a change. You don't look at the card that's dealt down until all the drawing and betting is over, so it's almost all guesswork.

Mr. Rake was the kind of card player who was too proud to fold, no matter how bad his cards were. And he was drunk. That happens a lot with fathers whose children die. Mothers take to drink, too, sometimes, but not so often as fathers. They think about how sad their dead children would be if they looked down from heaven and saw them drunk, so they hug their other children and cry, instead.

Between hands, I tried to tell Mrs. Rake the simple rules, but she shook her head and closed her mouth hard. The only thing she cared about was the fact that her husband was losing the family money. She looked so miserable, I thought she might throw herself into the river, with Emily in her arms.

Hands in Blind Blackjack go fast. Mr. Rake lost twenty-two dollars in quarters in less than fifteen minutes, and no end in sight. In the middle of the thirteenth game he stood up, put his empty glass on top of his cards, winked at his wife, and left to buy another bottle. As soon as he was out of sight, I sat down in his place and moved his empty glass off his cards.

Lies come to me with no trouble at all, sometimes two or three at a time. "Mrs. Rake told me to finish her husband's hand," I said. "I'm godfather to their daughter, Emily." Then I unbuttoned my shirt and took out my money pouch, and undid Clayton's side so Mr. Spellman could see the ten-dollar gold pieces, and laid it down with the open end facing him.

He leaned across the barrel, pretending to admire the daisy in my lapel, but really counting the gold pieces.

"I feel lucky," I said. "How do you play this game? It looks easy."

He leaned back and took his eyes off the pouch. "Easy as pie," he said. "Highest number up through twenty-one wins. Take however many cards down you want. Bet and look. It's all up to you. Win the heart of Lady Luck, the cards fall your way, and you walk away a rich man. Richer than you sat down, anyway. You old enough to play? I don't want to take advantage of a child."

"I'm older than I look," I said.

He looked around at the people watching. "I suppose I'll have to take your word for it. It ain't my fault if you're lying."

By drawing one card too many, I lost twenty-five cents right away, and then four quarters twice. On the fourth hand, I won a quarter back. I picked that coin up, waved it in the air, and stamped my feet on the deck. "This is the easiest game in the world," I said. Then I won a dollar, and I told Mr. Spellman I wanted to start betting my gold pieces, if he was up to it. What I was telling myself was that I was smarter than he was. In my heart, at that moment, I believed there really was a Lady Luck, and she was on my side, and I was going to double my money and cover myself with glory for the sake of poor Mrs. Rake and Emily. In short, my blood was up.

Mr. Rake came along with his bottle while I was dealing my first ten-dollar hand. Mrs. Rake stopped him, put Emily in his arms, whispered something in his ear, took the bottle out of his hands, and tipped it back in her own mouth. I never saw such a surprised look on a man's face in my life. She put the bottle behind her, pushed him over to the stairs, and sat down on his lap on the bottom step.

I won the first hand, so from being one dollar down I was now nine up. Then I lost two hands, won one, and lost three more. I was thirty-one dollars behind. Still, I was sure I was going to beat him. "One last hand for bigger stakes," I said. "I got people waiting dinner."

I put two gold pieces in the center of the barrel. Mr. Spellman looked in my face, took a little flask out of his shirt pocket, sucked down a gulp, screwed the lid back on, looked up at the sky as if he was worried, and covered me. I dealt one down and one up. My one up was a four. His was a nine. That made me bold, and I put down twenty dollars more and took a second card up. So did he. Mine was a Queen, his was an ace, which counts either one or eleven, player's choice. He bet ten more and called. We turned our cards over. My hand added up to twenty-five. He had twenty, a winner. I had lost eighty-one dollars. That finished me.

I took another gold coin out of my money pouch, hung the pouch back around my neck, got up, and went over to the stairs. Mrs. Rake was still sitting on her husband's lap to keep him down. As I went by them I slipped the gold piece to her. "Your share," I said, and kept going. On my way upstairs, I thought about the silver dollar I had thrown in the river, and I was almost sorry I had thrown it.

Dinner was good, but I couldn't keep my mind off what a fool I had been. Cécile asked me if I was sad getting near New Orleans, and I said yes, which was true. They knew I hadn't bought my ticket to France yet, and Dr. Gelineau asked me if I wanted him to try to get me a place on their ship, *L'Anémone*, which was leaving in two days.

"I still have money," I said. "You don't need to help me pay for it."

"Yes, yes, of course," Dr. Gelineau said. "You will absolutely pay for it. But it is a French ship, and perhaps I can talk to the Purser and find the best berth for you, for the least money. You won't have a cabin to yourself. All the more reason to want a window, if I can obtain one for you."

I told them they had done too much for me already, and I shouldn't ask them to do more.

Dr. Gelineau shook his head. "No. Not true. Many things in life a man *must* do for himself. If he has friends who enjoy helping him in the other things, he should allow them to have the pleasure."

I told him thank you, I'd be glad to have him see about it.

Just then Mrs. Rake came into the dining room with Emily behind her. Emily was in her nightdress. In her left hand she had a little white envelope. I worried that Mrs. Rake might have found out how the game had really gone, and come to give me back the ten dollars. I thought I might have to figure out a way to make her keep it, but I didn't need to.

Emily did a little curtsy, which was hard in her brother's shoes, and handed me the envelope. Inside was a piece of paper with "Thank you, Mr. Desant" written across it, and a drawing of a lilac bush at the bottom. All of a sudden, with her looking up at me, I didn't feel like such a hero. I saw that I hadn't done anything. As Mr. Henze says, money can't raise the dead, or make a stupid man smart, or a shrewish woman kind. It can't make a drunk husband sober, either.

Cécile invited them to sit down, but Mrs. Rake said no, thank you, it was Emily's bedtime. Then she grabbed my arm in a fierce way and pulled me to her and kissed me on the mouth. It was the first time a woman had ever done that to me, and I was sorry because I wanted Cécile to be the first.

After they left, we went outside to look around. There we were, in the middle of New Orleans harbor. The city was ten times as bright as Saint Louis is at night, and the Mississippi River was ten times wider, with boats anchored everywhere. The water there is a little bit salty from the ocean, and you get a good mixture of fish. There were boats of all sizes around us with their lanterns hanging out over both ends. The lights glittered off Cécile's black silk dress.

"Do you always give a gold piece away when you lose?" Dr. Gelineau asked.

I asked him how he knew about the game, and he said the head steward in the dining room had told him about a boy who had lost a hundred dollars in five minutes.

"It was less than a hundred, but it went fast," I said. "He cheated her husband. At least, I think he did. It was her money by rights."

We kept looking around the harbor for a while, and then Cécile said good night. Dr. Gelineau stayed with me. "You've done us a favor," he said. "You know that? Perhaps not. We lost a brother last April. Maurice. He and Cécile were not two years apart. They were best friends. She hasn't talked about him without crying since he died. Then today at lunch they served currants, which was his favorite berry, and she remembered picking them with him when they were children, and trying to count how many there were. You make her think of him in a happy way. So, if there is a debt between us, it is all on my side."

## XXI

## I DELIVER MR. NOWAC'S MINKS

I saw the LaMaire Import and Export Company even be-fore the *Lloyd Morris* docked. It was a big wooden building two hundred yards back from the dock from where they put the gangway down. Mr. LaMaire was there, and I gave him the sample mink and Mr. Nowac's letter. He read the letter straightway, not even looking at the mink, and when he was done reading he turned around in his chair, opened his safe, took out a tin box of money, and gave me fifty dollars. "For services," he said. "Mr. Nowac says that without you, his whole shipment would have been lost."

I didn't turn it down.

Cécile had told me I should go get a little present to bring Clayton. I wanted it to be something patriotic, so I bought him a tinted drawing of President Polk in a round silver frame the size of my hand that folded away. It cost only two dollars, and the frame was worth at least that much.

Dr. Gelineau had told me he would leave me a note down-stairs at his hotel to tell me if he'd gotten me a ticket on

*L'Anémone* or not. I stayed away from there until after dinner, afraid to find out that the ship was already full. When the clerk gave me an envelope with my ticket in it, I was so happy I figured I was halfway to saving Clayton. It was a very foolish idea.

That night and the next I slept in a twenty-five-cents-a-night hotel with a mate from a Brazilian ship and a traveling dentist. I was in the middle, but they both washed before they got into bed, and the dentist slept on his back all night, stiff as a board, with his toolbox between his feet to make sure nobody stole it. The bed was built for four, and with him so still, and the Brazilian pretty quiet, too, it was almost like having a bed to myself.

## XXII

# I STUDY FRENCH ON THE OCEAN

We steamed out of New Orleans harbor on March tenth. *L'Anémone* was twice as long as the *Lloyd Morris*, but only two feet wider. It had smokestacks plus two masts set into thick brass collars bolted to the deck, plus a bowsprit, and eight mainsails. Even with spark screens over the smokestacks to keep the sails from catching fire, and burning coal instead of wood, they were full of little burn marks. The paddles, with iron half-moon shields over the top of them, were on the sides. They pushed us day and night between four and five miles an hour, and when the sails were out in a stiff wind, we could go seven or eight.

Land was in sight most of the time for the first week. Then, after we were past the Keys of Florida, there was nothing but ocean for a month. Sometimes we would pass a ship going the other way, and the Captain would send up flags, and some of us would stand out on the deck waving, but then the ship would go over the horizon and we would be alone again. Halfway across we met a ship from the same Company and stopped and traded bags of mail. We had a half-hour warning, so I wrote a letter to Mama and Papa saying I was fine, and telling them all about the Gelineaus, and how Dr. Gelineau had cared for my snakebite, to show what good friends they were.

My ticket cost one hundred and ten dollars, which I paid Dr. Gelineau right away. He added forty dollars on his own so I could eat with them in First Class. All the tables sat six. Three old Frenchmen ate dinner and lunch with us, but it was always just the three of us for breakfast. One of the old men started paying court to Cécile the first day. I didn't understand anything he was saying, but I knew he was courting her, because sweet talk sounds the same in every language.

The night we were going through the Florida Keys it was windy and rainy, and when the waiter brought out ices the old man argued with him that they were too cold, and took off his silk scarf and tried to get Cécile to put it around her neck. She just smiled and folded it up and laid it down next to his plate. During coffee, Dr. Gelineau took a stroll with him around the dining room, talking seriously, and the man never tried to give her anything again.

Our first day out on the Atlantic, at lunch, I asked Cécile if she would go over my list of French words and tell me how to say them. After that, I went to her for a lesson every afternoon. She had a box full of her drawings from their trip through Old Mexico, and first thing she would take them out and we would go through them one by one. Most sheets had five or ten different drawings squeezed in every which way.

They were all in ink, and some of them she had colored during long train rides. Most of them were outdoor scenes, mountains, rivers, trees, and such. Not many had animals or people. She didn't think she could draw people's faces or animals' legs well enough.

I made all kinds of mistakes all the time, but she never acted like a schoolteacher with an ignorant student. I once said *âme*, which means "soul," instead of *âne*, which means "donkey." Then she laughed at me. She couldn't help herself, it was such a dumb mistake. Sometimes, after that, to get her to laugh, I would make a mistake on purpose.

After the drawings, we would walk up and down through the ship, and I would tell her where we were, and how quickly or how slowly we were going, and what we were passing by. When we had done our tour, we would find a place on deck where the smoke wasn't blowing and work on words and sentences I would need for asking strangers directions, and buying food or tickets, and renting a room in a hotel. The whole lesson, start to finish, would take about an hour and a half, and sometimes two. Then I would go back down to my deck and she would take a nap.

She took to putting letters under my plate at dinner, which made the old man who had been sweet-talking her look at me as if he wanted to kill me. The letters were on blue ship's stationery, with *"L'Anémone"* in gold on the envelope, and my name outside in her fancy hand. I answered every one. At first, half of my sentences began with *"en vérité,"* which means "truly," which I had learned from my French Bible.

She didn't say anything about it at first, but then she told me not to use it because it would make me sound ignorant and proud at the same time.

I wanted to learn at least fifteen new words every day so she wouldn't think she was a bad teacher. It was always around midnight when I began answering her letters. Most of the men in my cabin would already be asleep by then, so I would go to the *salon*, where they kept the lamps turned up full all night and I could look words up and read her letter and mine out loud, if nobody else was there.

Three days before we got to France, Cécile said she wanted to draw a picture of me reading. We were on the sunny side of the ship, so I was squinting a little, but she said that was good because it showed how serious I was. When she was done she said it wasn't good enough and so I couldn't look at it.

## XXIII

## CÉCILE WRITES ME A SERIOUS LETTER,
## AND WE GO THROUGH A STORM

Two days before we got to France, there was a storm. It started before lunch on April 12th with a hard west wind. Big waves began hitting us from the back and the left, sending up spray. We would heel over to the right, and then come back to center, and then heel over again. The sailors took in the topsails and tied everything down, chairs and tables and pianos. The wind kept blowing from the west, but the darkness was mostly in the south. Cécile and I did our French lesson sitting on tied-down chairs in the First Class library. The ship was rocking too much for us to walk around.

After dinner the wind suddenly dropped to almost nothing and the sky got clear, so we could go out and look at the sunset. The waves were still high, but we thought the storm was over and they would soon put the topsail out again, but they didn't. Just before dark, it started to rain. Cécile hadn't put a letter under my plate, and I thought it was probably because she had been packing or something, but as soon as we were inside, out of the rain, she gave it to me.

"This will take you longer to read than the others," she said. "It has no questions. It is a history I want you to know." Then she said good night and she and Dr. Gelineau went to bed. I went and got my dictionary and sat in the *salon* and read it. It was in as simple French as she could make it. Here is what it said:

*April 12, 1849*

*Dear Henry,*
*A year ago today, our dear brother, Maurice Gelineau, died. This is a history of that day for you.*

*The catastrophe occurred on the street in front of number 16, rue Colyse, Paris, France. It was a dark day. We expected rain. At noon there was a noise of people singing in the street. We went to the window. A mass of men with sticks and flags was marching on the rue Marboeuf. To see them better, Maurice went to the ground floor and walked across the street.*

*I stood by the window and looked out. Some policemen walked behind the mass of men. When the men arrived at the corner of the Champs-Elysées, they turned left toward the Monument Etoile, and Maurice came back across the street. From the time we were children, Maurice and I liked the rain. He was never afraid of thunder, so he stood in the door to enjoy it.*

*A soldier came down the street and said something to him. Maurice walked across the street to him. The soldier lifted his gun and shot him. Then he began to load his gun again. I could not unlock the window, so I put my arm through the glass and said, "Stop." Then I ran down to the street. The soldier was gone. Maurice had been pushed back by the force of the bullet and was lying on his side by the chestnut tree next to our door. He looked at me and smiled and began to speak, but he died.*

*This is the history of the last minutes of our good brother, Maurice. My brother Alexandre and I will keep his memory green as long as we live. May the Lord hold our brother to His Sacred Heart forever.*

*Cécile Marguerite Gelineau*

I wanted to write a letter back, but I didn't know what to say. Finally I wrote, "*Quel dommage,*" which means "What a shame," and slid it under her door. The storm was getting worse. I went to bed.

When I woke up, the ship was pitching back and forth. I couldn't see if the other men were awake or not, but I knew they had to be. The air had the smell of sulphur, because the engine crew was throwing wet coal into the furnace. I got out of bed. The floor of the cabin had always been cold, but now it was wet and sticky, too. There was a sharp crack, like a gun going off in my ear, and I thought for a second that the keel might have split open, but then I heard the same crack twice more, which relieved my mind. I tugged on the string of my money pouch to make sure the knot was tight. I must have been thinking that if we sank, I would be able to buy breakfast from some shark as he swam by.

I got dressed. The door was stuck, so it took me a long time to pull it open and get out into the hall, which was hotter than the room. I tried to pull the door shut behind me, but I couldn't. Finally Mr. Boffin, the only man in the cabin who wasn't French, yelled out, "Don't latch it!" and I left it banging. I felt along the wall to the end of the hall. *This is what it feels like to wake up in a coffin underground*, I thought.

*L'Anémone* has halls running from front to back on both sides, with stairs to the different decks at the ends, so you can go everywhere without having to go outside. There are lamps on the inside wall and windows on the outside wall for light, so when I got into the hall I could see. I stood there not knowing which way to go first, and then I got a picture in my mind of Cécile, dead, lying on the ocean with her black dress spread out. I ran along the hall and up to her door and stood there listening, which was stupid because there was so much banging and thumping and creaking going on, there was no way I could have heard her. I knocked hard.

"Yes?" she said.

"Are you all right?"

"Yes. Are you?"

"Yes. I'll come back. I just wanted to be sure. Don't worry."

I went out onto the deck. The wind was so loud it blew all the other noises away, which made it seem almost quiet.

There was a greenish light coming up from the water, and the sky was dark. I guessed it was raining hard, but I couldn't be sure because there was so much seawater flying.

I went to the front of the ship, holding on to the inside rail, and squeezed myself into a space at the corner between a fire-hose locker and an air shaft. That way I could see ahead, but also look back along the left side. The day before, when the storm started, there had been long rows of waves running up behind the ship and going past. Now there were waves coming straight at us. It was like being on top of a big wagon rolling across high hills, with dark, swampy valleys in between, except that the hills were moving all the time, trying to run over us, and the swamps were trying to suck us under. At the tops of the hills, smaller waves rose up and broke off and flew away, like steam blowing from a fast train.

As soon as we started to drop down into a valley, the sky disappeared, and there was nothing to see but the next hill. The wind would drop as you got down to the bottom, the way it does on land when you drive into thick woods, and as you crossed the bottom the water would move faster and faster under you, and you knew that if the front of the ship didn't start to lift, you were going to go straight into the next wave and not come up.

The only sail still out, the one to the bowsprit, was just rags, but even without sails the wind kept heeling the ship over to the right and holding us there until we got past the top of a wave, and then letting us come back level as we slid down the other side. Each time we heeled, the left paddle would come up out of the water and begin to flap on the surface, like a cormorant running across a lake to get up enough speed to fly. I was surprised it was still turning, but I knew that if it didn't the wind would blow us sideways and the next valley would swallow us up. While I was watching, a slat came off it, spun up into the air, hit the water fifty yards back, and disappeared behind us. That's when I saw how fast we were going.

Strong and deep-set as the masts were, I wondered if the tops would be broken, if not by the wind then by the boat itself every time it pitched one way or the other. Whenever I drew back into my cave and got the wind out of my ears, I could hear the masts creaking in their sockets.

I decided to try to find out if the storm was getting better or worse by measuring the height of the hills in front of us. My idea was to get a line of sight between the tip of the bowsprit and the horizon and measure whether the gap was getting bigger or smaller. It was a fool's job. The ship was moving up and down and from side to side at the same time, and there was no line between the top of a wave and the sky, so I gave up and began counting how long it took for us to get from the top of one swell to the top of the next, counting *One-Mississippi, Two-Mississippi,* and so on, but the times were all so different it didn't tell me anything.

The fact is, I already knew everything I had to know. If the swells got higher, or the wind at the top of them got worse, or the furnace got flooded, or the paddles broke, we would sink. If the swell went down, and the paddles kept turning, and the keel didn't come apart, and we didn't leak too much, we would stay afloat.

I wanted to see Cécile. I waited until the ship started to heel over again, so if I fell I would hit against the wall instead of going over the side, and then I came out from my cave and went through the first door I could find. The hall was full of people. I was soaking wet, as if a bucket of water had been poured over my head, so they stepped back and let me through. Going past the First Class dining room on the way to her cabin, I saw Cécile sitting at our table talking to her brother as if it were just an ordinary morning. She was wearing a blue dress with big wide sleeves, and a gold necklace, and she had her hair tied up with a white ribbon. It was the first time in my life that I had seen her not in black. Then I remembered that it was a year plus a day since their brother died. She had put her mourning dresses away.

She saw me and waved with one hand, holding on to the table with the other.

Seeing her like that, I knew we couldn't sink.

## XXIV

## A CELEBRATION WITH SONGS AND
## SPEECHES, AND THEN AN ARGUMENT

The storm ended fast. By sunset, people were walking around outside looking at the damage. There were pieces of wood, bolts, brass rings, and ropes everywhere, plus glass from broken windows. There was a three-foot-wide fish shaped like a bat, called a skate, jammed in under the anchor winch. It took four men to get him loose. When they finally did, they spread him out on a stick and hung him from the bowsprit like a flag.

The worst damage you couldn't see. The axle on the left-side paddle was bent, and they had stopped it. If they had kept it turning, it could have gotten hot enough to start a fire. So the right-hand paddle had to be stopped, too, or it would have sent us in a big circle. Seams under the waterline were leaking, which made the ship ride deeper in the water, but there was a big pump connected to the steam engine, and they kept it going all the time, so as the water ran in through the open seams they pumped it out over the side. Slowly, we began riding a little higher.

Wind had pushed rain into the furled-up sails, so when the men started to draw each one up again a ton of water dropped down onto the deck and shook the whole ship. After the first crash, nobody paid any attention.

The Captain was so happy that he put more tables and chairs, plus a piano, in the Second Class dining room, and invited everybody to eat cold dishes and drink champagne. One of the Third Class passengers was a piano tuner on his way home to Berlin, and he got the piano open and tuned it. After we ate, passengers sang songs and played concert pieces and recited poems and speeches from famous plays. Every performer got a lot of applause. One of the speeches was from a play called *Cromwell*, by the famous Victor Hugo.

The man who had recited the speech was sitting at the table next to us, and after he sat back down he got into an argument with the old man who was sweet on Cécile about what Victor Hugo would have done if he had been on the ship and it had started to sink. The reciter said that Hugo would have helped to put the women and children into the ship's boats, and then gone to the bridge and stood with the Captain singing patriotic songs until the waves covered them. The other man said that this was an idiotic insult to Mr. Hugo's good sense and knowledge of France. It would have made Hugo weep to do it, but he would have made a place for himself among the women and children and saved his own life because he was the greatest glory of French literature and politics.

After they had argued for a while, the old man asked Dr. Gelineau, as a doctor, what he thought Victor Hugo would have done. They didn't know that Mr. Hugo was one of his patients. Neither did I, until later. He just said, "*Mon ami, c'est égal. Nous flottons toujours,*" which means, "My friend, it's all the same. We're still floating."

Then he stood up and took Cécile's hand and brought her to the piano and she sang a French song. She always fidgets a little with her hands when she's up in front of people, and then realizes she's doing it and puts them behind her back. When the song was done she curtsied very slowly and got Dr. Gelineau to stand up and bow while she applauded him.

After they sat down again, I took a deep breath, said a prayer, and asked her for a lock of her hair. "Having it will help me speak French," I said.

"Then it is yours," she said.

## XXV

## I LAND IN FRANCE

There was no breakfast next morning, just buckets of coffee and baskets of salty rolls on a table on deck, but the rolls were good and the coffee was strong and hot. Everybody was out watching the harbor. A steward came around with papers to fill out for the customs men. I understood some of the questions, and the rest I guessed.

When we were halfway into the harbor, Dr. Gelineau and Cécile came down to my deck. Their uncle from Le Havre was going to meet them and take them to stay the night at his home before they came to Paris, to get them used to sleeping in a bed that wasn't rocking back and forth.

Dr. Gelineau had drawn me a map of Paris. Across the top he wrote, "*R.R.—Le Havre / St.-Germain / Paris*," so I would know the right route and where to change trains. He put lines under three streets, <u>rue Lemercier</u>, where Clayton's Chapel was, <u>rue des Martres</u>, where his hospital was, and <u>rue Colyse</u>, where their apartment was.

As we were getting close to the dock, he pointed out the

shed where the officials would stamp me in, and the building where I could turn American money into French money, and the place where I could catch a jitney to the railroad station. Then Cécile saw their uncle waving from behind a wooden fence, and began waving back, so we started to say goodbye.

"I am anxious, leaving you to go to Paris and be alone among those bad men in your brother's Chapel," Cécile said.

I was sorry I had told her what was worrying me. "Maybe I'm wrong about them," I said.

"No, I am sure you are not wrong. You must visit us soon, soon. We will be in Paris on the day after tomorrow."

"I will," I said.

Then she put a little box in my hand. I knew what was in it, so I didn't have to look. They both kissed me on the cheek, which is the French way, and went up to their deck.

The last five hundred yards to the dock took more than an hour. The dead paddles dragging in the water slowed us down, and there wasn't much wind. The slower we went, the harder it was to turn. When we got close enough we sent two small boats with ropes to the dock, and the French dockers winched us in sideways. The sun was hot. A lot of people went inside after a while, but I stayed out on deck. When we finally got tied up and they had put the gangways down, I was in no hurry to get off, so I was one of the last.

The signs on the ship had all been in French and English both, but the signs on the dock were just French, and walking along with the other passengers, all talking French and yelling out French to the people who were meeting them, I knew what it felt like to be a Chinaman landing in America.

It wasn't just the language. It was everything. The windows, and the hats the dockworkers wore, and even the springs and axles on the wagons were different shapes. The only thing that looked American was the clock, which was at the top of a green pole and was exactly like the one in the Saint Louis train station.

I stepped out of the crowd and set my watch. It was ten after one. I looked around for Dr. Gelineau and Cécile, who had gotten off way ahead of me. I didn't see them, which was a good thing. If I had seen them, I might have run after them and asked to come to their uncle's. I had to learn to take care of myself. I was hungry, but I decided to get to the train station before I ate.

The Customs Man asked me a lot of questions, and I gave him the same answer over and over: "*Je suis Américain. J'encontre mon frère in Paris.*" "I'm an American. I'm meeting my brother in Paris." He squinted at me for a while, and then he shook his head and signed my paper and said something about not spending American money. I went to the bank office at the street end of the dock and got twenty dollars' worth of French *livres*. Each of the customers in front of me stayed at the window after they got their money, counting it. I didn't know how much I was supposed to have, so I just moved off. Why would the bank teller try to cheat me, anyway?

I put the *livres* in my pocket, to have them ready, and went to where the jitneys to the railroad station were. I was the last one on, and nobody asked me to pay, so I think it was free. When I got to the station I bought a ticket, a loaf of bread, and a piece of cheese. The train left at two-fifteen. It was crowded. Railroad cars in France are better than ours. They're divided into little rooms with two long seats facing each other, with lots of room above for your luggage. I got to sit next to the window. I slept a little. After it got dark, the moon was so bright you could see which trees were in bloom.

There were lots of stops, but in the long straight in-betweens we went over twenty miles an hour. You'd think it would make you dizzy to go that fast, but it doesn't unless you lean out the window and look straight down, and you can't do that but a second, because then you get soot in your eyes.

It was four in the morning when we got to St.-Germain, and I got out and went into the station to find out where the Paris train left from. With the high ceiling, and gaslights all around, and tall windows on three sides, and the marble floor, it was like a palace. I had a ticket all the way through, but I got in the ticket line anyway to ask directions. The man behind the counter knew what I was saying, I think, but I didn't understand his answer. I went to the back of the line and got to him a second time, but I still didn't understand.

To get to the platforms you go under a high arch. Walking through, I saw that there was a blackboard bolted to it with all the cities and times, plus the track numbers. My train was in, but it was empty, and all the doors were closed. I went to the far end of the platform and watched them take off the switching engine and back in the locomotive. After that I just watched the other travelers and waited for the doors to open.

I began to think about Clayton. He had stood on this same platform in November, when it had been cold, and maybe raining. He had had enough money in his pocket to live in Paris for a while and still get home, and the memory of his dream with the Angel Gabriel speaking to him, but still, he had been all alone, without friends, with no map in his pocket, standing there thinking he was in the middle of the worst sinners in the world, all speaking a language he thought could rot his brain.

It made me think that maybe he would be glad to see me, and glad, too, to have a good reason to leave.

Alas, I was wrong.

## XXVI

## TRYING TO FIGURE OUT WHAT TO SAY TO
## CLAYTON, AND GETTING TO PARIS

The closer I got to Paris, the more I thought about how I could open Clayton's eyes.

Every preacher tries to get together a group of sinners who want to become saints. Clayton had his sinners. My job was to show him they wanted to stay sinners. But what if I was wrong? What if, in the time between him writing me and me getting to Paris, Clayton had made true True Believers out of Deacon George and all the rest? If he had done that, I'd have to be glad, give him the money I'd promised him, and go home.

*But*, I asked myself, was Deacon George likely to be the kind of man who would ever convert to anything good? My answer was no. In the Gospels, thieves and tax collectors convert, but schemers never do. Maybe Clayton's thieves had come to hate their line of work, but if they had, Deacon George probably was keeping their noses to the crooked grindstone anyway. In that case, my best advice to Clayton would be to take his men aside when Deacon George wasn't around and tell them to go home and become farmers or something. Of course, Clayton couldn't do that without knowing a few words of French, but maybe I could teach them to him.

Probably it was hog heaven for the whole gang of them, and I would either have to scare Clayton into going home, or persuade him that preaching in Saint Louis would be easier and more profitable. If those arguments didn't work, I could say Papa and Mama missed him. He would believe that, but he wouldn't go home because of it. It would be stronger telling him that Clemmy had started panting for him like a hound dog in July as soon as I told her about his success. That would have the advantage of being true, but giving him any more reason to want to marry Clemmy Burke was something I didn't want to do.

My last idea was to sing the praises of France every time I saw him. If I did that, he would have to start praising America, giving all the reasons he thought it was better, and that might lead him to become homesick, or make him think it was his patriotic duty to go home and leave the French to people like me who couldn't tell right from wrong.

I kept thinking about these ideas, and others, until I got to Paris. Back in Saint Louis I had thought the two cities would be a lot alike. They aren't. If you came at night and picked up all the buildings in Saint Louis, houses and factories and churches and everything, and carried them ten miles down the river, and laid them out any which way, the next morning the people would wake up, look out their doors, shrug their shoulders, walk around until they found their places of business, and forget where the city had been and how it was laid out before. Paris is too heavy and old to be moved, but if you did move it, the people would move it back stone by stone, even if it took them a century to do it, because the spot it's on is holy ground to them.

The trains on the St.-Germain line curve around from the west and come into Paris from the north. When you get near it, the city looks like a picture on the front page of a storybook, with church spires and copper roofs and buildings crowded all together. Centuries ago, there was a wall. It's all fallen down now, but you can still see the line of stones, and the turns in the wall where watchtowers were. There are farms all around on the outside. Farmers plow almost to the wall. The crops were just beginning to come up the day I got there. I think I saw rye, but it was just the first little sprouts, so I can't be sure.

The first thing you see inside the wall is a parade ground. It has some scrawny grass on it, but it's mostly chalk and mud. There are barracks and stables, and two long sheds where they keep cannons and gunpowder. There were soldiers marching back and forth, with a drummer boy beating time. While I was watching, one of the soldiers stepped in a hole, and the men behind him fell over and had to help each other up. The boy didn't stop drumming, however, and the sergeant waved his arms and jumped up and down. The last I saw, they were still trying to figure out who belonged where in the line.

On the other side of the parade ground the land slopes up the Montmartre hill, with windmills grinding grain and pumping water. Most of the mills are on the far side of the hill, so you can just see the tops of their sails. The water comes out of deep-dug wells that never go dry, which is one reason people decided to put the city there in the first place.

Just before you get to the Saint-Lazare Station you come to a tunnel. The train slows down, and you have to shut the window to keep out the smoke. As soon as you come into the open again, you're in the station. It's small, like a downtown bank, and sits right in the middle of a busy part of the city. There are six other train stations in Paris, and jitneys go between them all. When one of the jitneys gets filled up with people, with stacks of trunks and packages tied on top, you'd think it was bound to tip over, but it never does.

Paris paving stones are flatter than the ones in Saint Louis, not because they have better stones in France but because they've had such a long time to find good ones and wear them down. Some of the best streets are covered with what they call *asphalte*, black stuff made from coal oil, with little stones and grit in it. Other streets, especially the ones where people pulled up stones in the Revolution of 1848 to heave them at the soldiers, have been left rough to punish the people and remind them not to revolt. Of course, that only makes the people more angry and more ready to revolt again, even if it means being killed or sent into exile.

Only the best streets get regular shovelings. The day I got there, it hadn't rained for two weeks, so there was a lot of warm garbage and horse manure in the streets. They have water wagons going around the better sections of town every morning to damp down the dust, but by noon, if it's windy, which it was that day, it's flying everywhere. The water sort of freshens up the manure.

Paris isn't all palaces and monuments and opera houses. Most of the streets are full of old buildings that look as if they could fall down anytime, and empty lots, and factory yards with wooden shacks and sheds you could push over with one hand. If one caught fire, they're so dry and oily, they'd burn down in two minutes, but while they were burning you'd probably think that they were a public monument to something and had been blazing for a thousand years.

As I stood in the front door of the station, looking around, the church bells started ringing nine o'clock. Every neighborhood has its own church clock, but they all ring off at more or less the same time. Clayton likes to stay up late and sleep late, so there was no hurry to find his Chapel. I was glad of that, because I wanted to be sure I could find Cécile and Dr. Gelineau's apartment when I needed to. There was a storage office at the station where people could put their luggage for the day for only ten *centimes*, and that's what I did. Dr. Gelineau's map covered a lot of streets, so I went the long way around, walking south to the square they call the place de la Concorde, which has a gateway the size of a courthouse, west along the Champs-Elysées, which Cécile had told me was the most beautiful boulevard in the world, and then along to their apartment. The Champs-Elysées is four times as wide as anything in Saint Louis, with old trees on both sides and a park on the south that goes down to the Seine River.

I had never seen so many different kinds of carriages in

one place in my life as I saw on that street. There were tilburies looking like slabs of bent wood with wheels, barouches with velvet curtains, so the old ladies inside could look out with only their wrinkly eyes showing, and two-horse victorias with springs four feet long, the sides and tops polished and shining in the sun. In and out among them were men on horseback trying to find the quickest way through. When I got near my turnoff I saw two victorias racing each other, four people crammed onto the seat of each one, and two more on the floor, their feet dangling down, almost touching the street. Everybody seemed to be rushing to get somewhere, but most of the rigs turned around at the far end of the avenue and started back the other way, as if the street was a racecourse at a fair.

I turned right at the rue Colyse, and half a minute later I was standing in front of their building. It's stone, like all the other buildings on the street, five storeys high and twenty paces wide, with two apartments on each floor. Dr. Gelineau and Cécile have the right side of the third floor, with five big windows and a little balcony facing the street. Their apartment goes all the way from the front of the building to the back, so when there's a breeze in the summer, they get it. Out on the street there are chestnut trees. It was the end of their blooming season, so they were dropping little white petals onto the cobblestones.

A barouche and a wagon were passing each other when I got there, and when they were gone I went to the spot at the tree nearest their door where Maurice must have fallen when the soldiers shot him. The gutter was deep there, so his blood must have drained down and run into the muddy basin at the end. I pushed the dead flowers next to the kerb aside with my foot. I was sure I wouldn't see any bloodstains on the kerbstones. Time washes almost everything away.

Under the tree I couldn't see but one of their windows. I had to go across the street to see the rest. I imagined Cécile's arm coming out through the end one, cut and bleeding, with blood dropping down. I could hear her voice yelling at the soldier to stop. While I was looking, two soldiers came up the street with guns on their shoulders. I wanted to walk away from them, but I didn't want them behind me so I walked straight toward them and looked them in the eye. My idea was that if they stopped me I would tell them that I was a friend of Dr. Gelineau's and on my way to the hospital to see him, which was half true, so they wouldn't think I had come to Paris to start another revolution.

After I found the hospital, which along with the nunnery where the sisters live and a big garden in between takes up a whole block, I walked around it. Then I went back to the railroad station, picked up my valise, and went to find Clayton's Chapel.

## XXVII

## CLAYTON'S CHAPEL

Rue Lemercier, Clayton's street, is wide enough for two wagons to pass with plenty of room to spare, but the side streets are more like alleys, and turning a wagon into one means the driver has to go up onto the kerb. Wagons stop and unload, or wait for the wagons in front of them to move, and people have to walk around them. There's muck everywhere, so you can slip and slide, and you do a lot of jumping. All in all, it's best not to be in a hurry.

The rue Lemercier is about a half-mile long. When last year's Revolution started, people built two barricades across it, one halfway along and the other at the end, at the same time prying up cobblestones to throw, and it was never laid properly again, so the street near Clayton's Chapel is rough. There are bullet scratches and chips on some of the build-ings, and some broken windows that haven't been fixed yet. The top corner of the building where the first barricade had been built is gone. The street curves a little to the left, but it's straight enough for the cannons to get a clear shot. People say it's a miracle there was no fire.

Everybody, almost, drinks, but not whiskey. Sometimes a man will get coffee on his way to work, if he has a job, which half the men don't, and put brandy in it, but most of the drinking is wine, so they don't get drunk the same way they do in Saint Louis. They take their time at it. You can't go into a café or a tavern and come out staggering five minutes later and fall under the wheels of a wagon. Also, none of the men carry guns, unless a revolution is going on.

At the corner of the rue de Moncey, which is the cross street before Clayton's Chapel, there was a drunk asleep, with his legs sticking out into the gutter. A wagon turning that corner would have crushed them, but nobody paid any attention to him. I was afraid if I stopped to move him someone would think I was trying to rob him, so I went around him the same way everyone else did.

Halfway along the next block was Clayton's sign, hanging from an iron bar high out over the street. It wasn't as big as I thought it would be, but it was white, with red and blue lettering, so you couldn't miss it. Clayton believed that preachers who called themselves Doctor and had names starting with an initial got more respect. His favorite initial was "W," standing for "Winner," and there it was.

AMERICAN CHAPEL!
AMERICAN PREACHING!
THE REV. DR. W. CLAYTON DESANT

I put down my valise and stood in a doorway across the street and looked at the chapel. It was made of brick, with a big oak door in the center and an alley running down the left-hand side to a yard in back. The ground-floor bricks facing the street had been scrubbed and the door handle polished. It looked nice.

The bells on the church one street over and two streets up rang three o'clock, so I knew Clayton would be awake, but I just kept looking, waiting to see what there was to see. After a while, the door opened and a man came out. He was tall, with little black eyes set close together. The bottom part of his left ear was missing, and a tiny black beard was poking from the end of his chin. "That's *Deacon George*, for sure," I said to myself, and I stepped back into the doorway so he wouldn't notice me, and watched him walk away the way I had come.

After he was out of sight, I decided to go rent a room at a hotel before I saw Clayton, and pay a week's rent in advance, so that if he offered me a bed upstairs when I came back, I would have a reason to say no.

Two blocks farther on was the Hôtel Marianne, and I went to it. I knew it would be cheap the minute I walked in, because it had oil lamps and tallow candles instead of gaslights. The landlady, Madame Forché, who did all the work except scrubbing the floors, was sitting behind her desk with a cloth in her hand, polishing a brass lamp. I couldn't get myself to ask her to let me see the privies, so I took the fact that she kept the brass clean as a sign that everything else would be clean, too.

For a second I couldn't remember the word for "week," so I asked for seven days. I did remember "small room on the top floor," though I had to repeat it. She put down her cloth and looked at me. I told her I was an American. She smiled and nodded her head. "Lafayette," she said, remembering the Frenchman who had saved our Revolution. I took the French money out of my pocket and held it out for her. She put down her rag, wiped off her hands on her apron, picked out some coins, and led me upstairs. When we got in the room, she opened the window and pointed to the café across the street and told me I could get breakfast there. Then she left me alone. I wasn't sure if she meant it came with the price of the room. It didn't.

I had fetched bodies from hotel rooms when I was working for Mr. Henze, but except for New Orleans I had never paid money to a hotel in my life. That was just for a bed, and this was a whole room. I grabbed the counterpane and pulled it back fast. No bugs ran away, and the sheets didn't look dirty, so I felt right at home. Also I was three storeys up, so the breeze through the window smelled better than the air down on the street.

My clothes were damp from the trip, so I spread them out on the bed and the bureau, hung my suit on the hanger behind the door, put my gift picture of President Polk into the sun to dry out, and sat down in the chair by the window. Two and a half blocks away I could see Clayton's sign gleaming over the street, and his front door, too.

On the street in front of the hotel was a coal wagon. I could have leaned out and spit straight down and hit it. There was a delivery wagon in front of it, trying to turn into the alley just past the hotel, and two wagons behind it, so there was no way to go ahead or back up. All it could do was creep ahead two or three feet every time the wagon in front did.

The horse moved every time he had the chance, but the driver whipped him anyway, even if he had already started to pull. If it had been night, I would have seen sparks from under his iron shoes every time he heaved.

A skinny boy came along the street from behind. He had a knife in his fist, with the point poking out past his thumb, glinting in the sun. When he got to the back of the wagon, he reached up and slashed one of the bags. Coal started dropping down onto the street. He put the knife in his pocket, and when he came up next to the driver he waved and pointed to the street, where the coal was bouncing. The man jumped down. Before he was halfway to the back the boy had grabbed a sack from the front and was putting it on his shoulder. As he was getting it balanced he looked up and saw me watching him. He didn't move. He just stood there, waiting to see if I would betray him by yelling "Stop, thief!" I could have, but he wasn't stealing a poor man's money, or knocking anybody over the head, so I kept still. After four or five seconds he saluted me with his free hand, walked across the street as if he was making a delivery, wove in and out through the crowd, and turned left into an alley. He never looked back, but I knew he would remember my face if he ever saw me again, and I would remember his.

I ran down the stairs and helped the driver finish packing his coal into another sack, and then I went to the end of the alley into which the boy had turned. I thought it would run all the way through to the next street, but it was a dead end full of children and junk, with apartments all around. I wondered which one the boy had gone into.

After a minute, I decided it was time to go and see Clayton, so I went back up to my room to fetch the picture of President Polk, and went to the Chapel of Thieves.

## XXVIII

## I SEE CLAYTON

The window in the Chapel door was ripply orange glass, but it was clean and you could see through it. The room was big, with lamps along the walls, all of them lit. Clayton was standing in front of the altar. Between him and the first row of chairs was a lit candle on a candlestick. In the far corner was a half-open door with a stairway going up to the second floor.

Deacon George was sitting in the next to the last row of chairs, with his back to me.

I opened the door and went in. Clayton was preaching, so he didn't notice me, but Deacon George heard the door and got up right away and came over to me with his hand out. His palm was shiny wet. "I saw you an hour ago," he said. "You were across the street. Spying?" He shook my hand and kept hold of it.

"Just looking," I said.

"You have removed a great burden from my mind. I thought you might be a thief. A man alone must be on his guard day and night. Evil is around every corner in this city." He called out to Clayton without turning around. "Reverend Doctor! Your brother is here." Then he gave my hand a last squeeze and let go, making a sucking sound.

Clayton came up the aisle. He was pale and a little fatter, but he looked fine. "Henry, what are you doing here?"

I took his present out of my pocket. "I brought you this," I said. "It's a tinted picture of President Polk."

"Thanks." He looked at it and put it on a chair. "Just for your information, Henry, I don't need to be told who the man in the picture is. I know my President when I see him. I'm still one hundred and fifty percent American. What do you want me to do with it?"

"I thought you might hang it on the wall over your bed, or put it on your desk or something. It got a little damp during a storm, but the frame isn't warped at all."

He picked it up and sighted along the top edge. "Seems square enough. How come you're here?"

"I found money in Aunt Minna's chimney clock. I wrote you a letter saying I was coming here with your half."

"Chimney clock? You know the word for 'chimney clock' in French?"

"No."

"Neither do I, but I don't need to. Tell him, Deacon George, what's French for 'chimney clock'?"

He squinted and made his small eyes even smaller. "*Horloge de cheminée.*"

"Hear that, Henry? A preacher who goes to a foreign country and allows himself to be led by the Spirit to a helper like Deacon George don't need to know a single native word. My Deacon knows *three thousand English words*. Count them! Plus three thousand French ones, plus fifty Polish ones for good measure. What do you think of that?"

"Those are good round numbers," I said.

"I knew Auntie had money hidden away somewhere! Didn't I tell you so at the cemetery? How much?"

"Your half is a hundred."

"Only two hundred total? Don't you believe it, Henry. There's more there you could have sniffed out. The Lord rejoices to see His Children prosper. It's good to have goods. It's only Satan wants us to be poor. You sure it was no more than two hundred? A tight-fisted old lady like that surely laid by a heap more. You should've kept on looking. Under the floorboards would have been a good place to start."

"You're the one who should look. You hunt ten times better than I do. Remember that tin of French jellies for your birthday?"

"Don't bring it up. Still makes my stomach turn to think of it. Is the money in gold? Give it here."

I took my money pouch out and put ten ten-dollar pieces in Clayton's hand. He counted them twice and put them in his pocket.

"You get my letter?" I said.

Deacon George smiled at me. "We received your letter two days ago. The Reverend Doctor Desant hasn't seen it yet. He has the Lord's work to do and is not to be annoyed with small things. Have you bought your ticket home? I can buy one for you today right here in Paris. You must long to return home safely. Paris is a dangerous city if you have no friends."

I was about to say I had Paris friends, but I didn't want him to know.

"I don't have much truck with mail these days," Clayton said. "Deacon George does all my hauling and fetching. Sodom and Gomorrah? Them heathen cities in the Bible? They probably had a hundred post offices, the same as Paris. How much good do you think all those post offices did for the citizens of those sinful cities when the Lord came down upon them in His wrath? None at all! You ever read about Jeremiah going to the post office to mail a prophecy to the people of Israel? Well?"

"No," I said.

"Doggone right. Come to think of it, now, how much do you suppose an original Sodom and Gomorrah postage stamp would be worth in ready money today? Plenty, I can tell you. But my point is, if you found one, there wouldn't be no Prophet's handwriting on the envelope. You say Saint Paul the Apostle wrote letters? Well, that's true, but that was New Testament times, which is different from Old Testament times. He's one of *us*. By the way, we got no bed for you here. You'll have to find a hotel."

"I got one. Right up the street."

"You sure it's a hotel and not some house full of Shady Ladies and other Evil Doers?"

"It says 'Hôtel' on the outside."

"Maybe 'hôtel' in French don't mean the same thing as 'hotel' in English. Ever think of that? Don't let them cheat you on the price. Anyway, I got something I can do I want to show you. Follow me to the altar. Any fool can preach. You could, probably. Well, maybe not. Because mere words ain't enough. You got to say the right words with potency and positive power, and that means you got to have the right Spirit coming behind exploding letters. I'll show you. Stand back now, or you'll get a face full of hot wax."

I went back behind the second row of chairs.

He lined up his head with the candle and took a deep breath. "Flee Pagan People Promoting Popish Pageantry!" he said. With each $P$, the flame shook, but the candle stayed lit. He moved half a step closer and took another deep breath. "Flee the Pestilential Prod of Punishment Perpetual!" When he said the word "Prod" the candle almost went out, and with the second $P$ in "Perpetual," it did.

He smiled at me. "See? Potent $P$'s."

The Deacon struck a match and lit the candle again.

Clayton cleared his throat. "What's my secret, you want to know? Three things: no truck with Demon Tobacco, plus Practice and Prayer, two more $P$ words, if you'll notice, like 'Patriarch' and 'Prophet.' The letter $P$ is the most Powerful of all letters, after $G$, $J$, and $C$, of course, plus $H$. What do you say, Henry? Have I got the truth by the tail?"

"You know how to get the wind going," I said.

He leaned into the flame and said, "Prophet," and it went

out. Then he pulled me over to Deacon George. "This lucky little boy heard my very first Sermon. At a bunny rabbit's funeral. Can you believe that?"

"I'm sure it was a blessing to him," Deacon George said.

"Ha ha ha. To Henry, or the bunny? Which, George?"

"To Henry, certainly, but if bunnies had souls, you would have sent that lucky beast straight to Heaven."

Clayton punched me in the arm in a friendly way. "As any fool can plainly see, the Deacon's a man of great spiritual discernment."

I asked him if I could see the rest of the building. He shook his head. "Sorry, Henry. Look around down here as much as you want, but it's only me and Deacon George and the True Believers allowed upstairs. Nothing up there somebody like you would want to see, anyway. Steep stairs around in back you could fall down and hurt yourself on, a big table with pages and pages of sermons on it you wouldn't understand, not in your present ignorant state."

"If I just peeked through the door I could write a letter and give Mama and Papa an idea of what the whole place looks like."

Clayton shook his head. "Too late. Already wrote to them and done it. The fact is, Henry, I got a very private record book up there where I write down all the various offerings we get. That way, the whole world can see that I'm the shepherd of a generous and resourceful flock. It's Deacon George's idea. I say, give the Lord all the credit, but he says no, I should get some, too, and I suppose he's right. Then there's all those loose sermon sheets on the table. You'd open the door and they'd fly every whichaway."

"Maybe I can see it next week?"

"You expect to stay that long?"

I didn't want to say how long I'd stay. "I did what you told me I should in your letter," I said. "I went to Clemmy's house and talked about your success."

He smiled a big, happy smile. "Henry, if that girl could be in this holy place and hear me preaching in my full power, like you're going to see and hear me tonight, she'd jump under our porch and scratch in the dirt like a dog, trying to find that ring I gave her."

"If she fit," I said.

"You'll be going home soon, and I want you to bring her a gift from me. I'd put it in the mail, but you can't trust these Frog postmen. Little square hats, India-rubber stamps. Pagan frumpery, I say. A three-layer box of genuine Swiss chocolates from Switzerland. Stupid name for a country. One of my Flock brought it in just last night. Deacon George sells most things and gives the money to the poor, but some things you can't get a fair price for, and used chocolates is one of them. How did she look? The same bouncing girl she always was?"

"She's pining for you, Clayton, I can tell you that. But there's other men hot on her trail, hoping to win her heart away from you."

He shook his head. "It's a pity, Henry, how she went and lost my affection. It was all your fault, of course, writing that book."

"Mention your name and she pants like a hound dog in July," I said. "There's going to be a big party on her front porch the day you get back, I can tell you."

"I know. Panting and Pining for me, two more *P* words. Power, Henry, Power."

## XXIX

## I SEE CLAYTON ALONE

I asked Clayton if he wanted to go down the street and get a piece of cake. He opened his mouth to say yes, but Deacon George jumped in.

"We find our time precious in the extreme, Henry. The Reverend Doctor Desant has been delivering, to his faithful flock, a splendid series of sermons on the Ten Commandments. Tonight is Tuesday. He speaks on Commandment Number Eight, *Thou Shalt Not Steal.* French Priests call it Number Seven, but they are all of them peasants, as well as Slaves of Satan."

"Deacon George knows the enemy," Clayton said.

The man shrugged his shoulders. "You are too good, Reverend. This afternoon, I will go to the baker and buy your favorite cake, apricot and chocolate. Once you have delivered tonight's sermon, and I have sent the Faithful out to harvest offerings, you can feast to your heart's content."

I put my hand in my pocket and took hold of the box with the lock of Cécile's hair, for courage, and looked Deacon

George in the eye. "I have to talk to my brother about family business," I said.

He smiled. His teeth were small, like baby teeth. "So be it. The Fifth Commandment tells us, *Honor Thy Father and Mother*. We are open of heart. Aunts and Brothers have their place, too."

I left and went outside. Clayton followed me. As soon as we got across the street, he said, "I want you to know, Henry. Apricot and chocolate ain't my favorite cake. They don't mix. Deacon George thinks it is, and I don't want to hurt his feelings."

"That's very nice of you."

"I do all of the virtues, Henry. Let's get to business. I know what you're going to say, that Mama and Papa want me to come home and work on Aunt Minna's farm."

"I don't think so," I said.

"Well, I'm not going to do it. I wasn't put on this earth to spade up dirt, spread manure, and poke pigs with sticks."

"I know."

"Aunt Eusie change her will? Is that it? She owes us. We gave her the whole of our summer last year, going up and down the Missouri, all for nothing."

"Nobody's changed anything, as far as I know. I need to tell you something."

"Go ahead."

"Your Flock is all thieves, and Deacon George is ten times worse than the rest. I could tell from your letter. Everything they bring in? They're not offerings, they're stolen goods. You've got to get away from them."

"I didn't write you that."

"Still, it's true."

He bit his bottom lip, looked down, and rubbed his right shoe on the back of his left pants leg. "You're jealous of me, Henry. You've always been that way. Whatever I have, you want."

"I don't want what you have," I said.

"Well, good, because you ain't going to get it. You'll be sitting in the pew listening to me tonight?"

"Sure. I'll wear my good suit and everything. You ought to think about what I told you."

"Just don't walk in looking like an undertaker come to fetch away a body, is all."

"I won't shame you, Clayton."

"My preaching will open your eyes, Henry. Sunday I gave it to them with both barrels on the subject of Commandment Nine. If I'd known you were coming, I'd have waited so you could hear it. You ought to know Number Nine. It's for liars. *Thou Shalt Not Bear False Witness*—does that ring a bell?"

"I know the Commandments."

"Credit where credit is due, Henry. You brought me my hundred dollars. You could've just put it in the mail and saved us both the trouble, but you didn't, you brought it to me instead. It was a useless waste of your time and mine, but it was a kindly act, and I thank you for it."

"You're welcome."

"But that don't give you no rights over me. You found them gold pieces by pure luck. Don't think you can wedge me out of my Chapel just by bringing me what's already mine by rights."

"It's a lie," I said.

"It's the God's honest truth, is what it is."

"No, I mean what I told you about Aunt Minna's clock. There's nothing in there but broken innards. I unscrewed the back when I went to say goodbye to Papa and Mama. That money I gave you is mine, out of my bank account."

He put his hand in his pocket and felt the coins. "Ain't true. If it was, they'd feel hot."

"I lied about the money so Deacon George would have an extra reason to keep you out of jail until I got here."

Clayton shook his head. "If you knew how I suffer every day, you wouldn't torture me like this, Henry. It's a fiery trial for a True Believer like myself to live in a city filled with sin. If you knew how hard it is for me here, you wouldn't try to scare the daylights out of me."

"That isn't what I mean to do."

"What you mean to do, and what you don't mean to do, don't mean nothing to me. You want to know what sorts of corruption I have to witness every time I go out on the street? Look at that Shady Lady coming this way on the other side." He pointed to a girl about sixteen carrying a wooden box full of shoelaces and ribbons to sell. Her dress was cinched up to keep it out of the filth. "See that shameless Jezebel? Ankles bare for every man to see? Public nakedness is what it is, nothing less. That old man sliding along behind her? Probably stole the lot, and now he won't let her out of his sight, for fear she'll cheat him."

"Is that what Deacon George told you?"

"I don't need him to tell me such things, Henry. I was born with an eye for sin."

"Maybe he's her daddy or her uncle, watching out to see that nothing bad happens to her."

"You go ahead and believe that if you want. I know the both of them. They come traipsing into my Chapel my first week here. Said something in French to me. Some lie, naturally. They just wanted to get in out of the rain. Left as soon as the storm let up. Saved me the trouble of cleaning them out like Jesus cleaned out the moneychangers."

"She looks nice. Maybe they wanted to hear you preach."

Clayton shook his head. "Shady Ladies come in all sizes and ages, Henry, but not one of them has ears for the truth. They're sly. They don't all dress up in scarlet silk. So if you come to a bad end because of one, don't call me to your deathbed and say I didn't warn you. I got to go now. Service is at eight. My Flock comes downstairs on time, so don't you shame me by being late."

He walked back across the street. I didn't want us to part with angry words, so I followed him. When we got inside, Deacon George was sitting in the last row again, cleaning his fingernails. "My brother says our Flock is all thieves," Clayton said as soon as he shut the door.

Deacon George didn't even look up. "Is that what you think, Henry? Who told you?"

"Nobody."

"You saw it spying from across the street?"

"No. I know what's going on, is all," I said.

He looked at Clayton and shook his head slowly. "As you have said many times, Reverend, the true Prophet is never given due honor by his own flesh and blood. This boy may someday come to see your holiness, and ask for your forgiveness. He may even ask for mine. I will pray that he does. In the meantime, we both forgive him of our own free will."

"Amen," Clayton said. "He's a good boy. A hard worker, too, I'll give him credit for that."

Deacon George got up off his chair and came over and put his face close to mine and felt all over my head with his damp hand. "A born heterodox. I can tell from the shape of his skull. You must try to overcome Doubt, my son, or you will burn for all eternity. But enough of this pleasant conversation. The time has come for your brother to go upstairs and meditate on his sermon, which is only a few hours away."

"I know what you are," I said.

He went back to cleaning his nails, and I left. On my way to the café I caught up with the shoelace girl and bought some, and while I was eating, I put them in my shoes. I was due a change. My old ones were all worn out.

## XXX

## CLAYTON PREACHES A SERMON
## ON STEALING

I got to the Chapel ahead of time. The door was locked, so I looked in the window. It was empty, with none of the side lamps lit. I went down the alley toward the back. Halfway along the side of the building there were two big windows with bars. In between, an iron ladder ran up to the roof. I thought about climbing it to see if there was a skylight I could peep through, but I didn't want to get my suit full of rust and make Clayton even more ashamed of me than he already was.

In the back yard there was an old wooden shack lying on its side, and some broken tables and chairs, plus washtubs and bottles and other junk. At the corner of the fence was a pile of broken pipes. I went over the pipes and climbed the fence and followed the alley down to the next street. Then I turned right up to the rue Louis, where St.-Jean Church is.

From the top of the church steps, I could see the tracks of the St.-Germain line. There was a train chugging into the tunnel. The cars were lit up, and passengers were standing and taking down their luggage. Tomorrow morning, Dr. Gelineau and Cécile would be coming into Paris that way. I kept watching until the train had gone out of sight, and then I went into the church. It was much bigger inside than it looked from the outside. I went to the altar and knelt down and prayed for Clayton to be released from the power of Deacon George. I also tried to pray for Deacon George, but every time I shut my eyes to do it, all I could see were his little baby teeth and his pointy beard moving up and down as he talked, so I quit.

There was a beautiful marble statue of Mary high up in the side wall. Her dress was sky blue, with big sleeves, like the one Cécile had worn the morning of the storm. I went over and looked at her, thinking she might have something to tell me. After a while I heard footsteps behind me, and a Priest tapped me on the shoulder and told me he would be ready to hear my confession at eight. I took that to be the signal for me to go.

I ran to the Chapel, and got there in plenty of time. The lamps were all lit and the place was bright. There were seven men in the front row on the left-hand side, and two rows of four men on the right. I sat on the left, halfway back. The men didn't look like robbers, at least not the kind you see in magazine drawings. They all had new haircuts, so I could see their ears. Two of them were old.

In the clean windows you could see reflections of the lamps. After a while, Deacon George came down the middle aisle. When he got to the altar, he turned around and lifted his hands, and the congregation stood up. Then Clayton walked in, wearing a flowing black robe with a red silk lining. He looked like a bishop.

He said a long prayer, and then everybody sat down. One of the old thieves stood up, took a violin out from under his chair, and played a sad melody. When he was done, Clayton gave another prayer, opened up his Bible, and read through all the Ten Commandments. Then he repeated Number Eight twice, and started in preaching, taking turns with Deacon George. Clayton would talk for half a minute, and then Deacon George, behind him, would talk a little longer, in French.

Our Reverend back home, Mr. Pewbrace, can preach a powerful sermon, but Clayton is ten times better, even with stopping every half-minute. He began by telling a story about a thief who stole a mare with her saddlebags full of merchandise and got drowned trying to swim her across the Mississippi to Tennessee. The man had tried to pull off his boots and swim to shore, calling out to the mare to come back and help him, but she had swum away free, and Satan had sat laughing on the shore. After the man went under for the third time, Satan snatched his soul out of the water and carried it to hell.

"Every thief is like that thief," he said, "doomed to burn forever in Eternal Fire, if he don't repent and change his ways."

If I had been a thief, I would have gone down onto my knees right then and cried out for forgiveness and amendment of life.

I don't know how exactly Deacon George translated what

Clayton was saying. He said the word *éternel* every time Clayton said "eternal," but he never said *feu*, which is "fire." They both said "merchandise," which is almost the same word in both languages, and they both gave long lists of what men could steal. The last on Clayton's list of merchandise was "a woman ripe for marriage." When he said the word *Femme*, Deacon George smirked and stroked his little black beard and smiled with his tiny teeth.

The robbers paid attention to both speakers, leaning forward in their chairs and tilting their heads this way and that, and from time to time one of them would shout out an "Amen!" Each "Amen" made Clayton smile and say thank you and ask for another, and he always got it.

The double sermon went on until almost ten o'clock. When it was over, Clayton lifted his hands in the air and blessed everybody. Then he went to the corner and opened the door and went up the stairs, and Deacon George led his men to the back, whispered to them, and sent them out the door. When they were all gone, he went to the bottom of the stairs and called for Clayton to come down and have a treat. He took some plates and forks and a knife, plus a big cake, out of a box in the corner, and sliced a piece for each of us. I had never eaten chocolate and apricot together before. It was a lot better than I'd thought it would be, and it's now one of my favorites.

While we were eating, I told Clayton what a good sermon it was.

"See? I told you," he said, and he began to punch me on the shoulder the way he used to back home. It was as if we were friends again. While we were eating a second piece of cake, I asked him if he'd like to walk back to my hotel with me and see my room.

"Not alone!" Deacon George said. "At night? Think about the danger for a moment, Henry. He would have to return along these dark streets by himself. No. Never! He is too modest to tell you, but every evil man and Shady Lady in Paris hates him. Already the whole city knows what he said tonight about robbers, and every evil person in this evil city is gnashing his teeth. There are men, and women too, outside in the street right now who would give their eyes to bring him to harm. No. We three will walk together to your hotel, and on the way back I will protect him."

We left. Opening the door I almost knocked down an old man who was standing in the doorway. "*Pardon, monsieur*," I said. He said something back and started to walk away, and I said, "*Merci*."

"How much of French you know?" Clayton said after we started walking along.

"Some words," I said.

"Warning, Henry. You start learning a foreign language, and sure as shooting you start losing your own. It's a true fact. Ask Deacon George, if you don't believe me."

"Your brother is correct, as always," Deacon George said. "Gain a French word, and you lose an American word."

"See? And the worst is, you don't know it's happening until it's too late. Here's how it works. A man is born with six thousand word slots in his brain. It's like birds' nests in a tree, one bird to a nest. You start filling them up when you're just a bitty baby, one word at a time. Even a little word like 'no' takes up a whole nest. You understand so far?"

"I think so."

"Good. Now listen close and give me your whole attention. When you start in learning to talk, it's like these little birds were getting out of their nests and flying around and landing back home again. But now comes the dangerous part. You leave America, let's say, and go to France, and after a while you get careless. You let a foreign word into one of your nests. Right away an American word gets pushed out. Just flies away, doesn't even say goodbye. Deacon George had to let all but fifty of his Polish words fly away for French ones after his wicked younger brother, the Upstart Prince of Warsaw, tried to murder him. Then, when agents of the Prince sent to track him down found him here, he had to flee to England and trade in half his new French words for English ones."

"It was destiny," Deacon George said. "God led me to England to prepare me to serve your brother."

"Learn a French word," Clayton said, "and an American word flies away, and you never see it again. The lesson is, if you go to a foreign country, keep a tight hold on your ignorance. Deacon George has a special gift. He can pick and choose what nest to throw a bird out of, so when he finds a good new English word, he can trade it in for some useless French one."

"Like what?"

"How do I know? They're all useless as far as I can see."

"That means Deacon George has three thousand English

words and two thousand and nine hundred and fifty French words, plus fifty Polish ones. Is that it?"

"Not exactly," Deacon George said. "Two thousand nine hundred French. I have retained a hundred Polish words, so that I can write home to my mama, the Dowager Queen."

"Clayton said fifty."

"Even the Reverend Doctor Desant can make small mistakes with numbers."

"Clayton told me in his letter you were a Prince, but I didn't know your brother wanted to kill you."

Deacon George smiled. "Not anymore. He has discovered that I am under Divine Protection, and has stopped even trying. My father, the former King, is now dead, and Prince Zoftig is wearing the crown. I forgive him. Why should I care? He must spend his life ruling over a land of peasants, and then die and go into Eternal Fire, while I am here serving Doctor Desant, with the promise of Heaven in the end."

"Listen to him," Clayton said. "See what a word master he is?"

## I AM KNOCKED DOWN IN THE STREET

When we were a block away from the hotel, I heard somebody running at us from behind. I turned around just in time to see the coal thief flying through the air at me. I could tell from the look on his face just before we crashed that he remembered me, too.

I thought he would fall down with me, but he kept his feet, took a hop and a skip, slid across the cobblestones like an ice skater across ice, and kept going. I didn't see him turn into his dead-end street, but I knew that was where he was heading. Some people gathered around to help me, but Deacon George pushed them away and grabbed my feet and dragged me backward through the muck. Then he pulled me up by my collar and wiped his hands on my shirt.

"You have not done yourself an injury, I trust?" he said.

I opened my mouth to tell Clayton I had seen the boy before, but he thought I was going to spit some muck his way, and jumped back, so I wiped my mouth instead of talking.

"You didn't break any bones, did you?" Deacon George asked me.

My left arm felt sticky inside my sleeve, so I knew it was bleeding, but nothing was dribbling out. The coal thief had hit me with his elbow under my left eye, and it was starting to swell, but I could see fine. "Nothing bad," I said.

I felt something wet and squishy in my fist, probably a wad of maggots. I didn't want to look at it, so I just flipped it onto Deacon George's pants. It made him jump back and growl like a dog. Then I walked up and down and swung my arms and bent forward and back. "Nothing's broken," I said.

Clayton shook his head. "You see now how it is in France, Henry? They're all barbarians."

"Your brother is right," Deacon George said. "When an innocent person is attacked in the street, he should think of going home right away."

"I'm fine," I said.

"It probably wasn't him that was the target," Clayton said. "That Demon was probably after me. I saw his face all black, like he had been shoveling coal to feed the Furnaces of Hell."

"Of course you are right, Reverend," Deacon George said. "And in order to save you for higher work, God turned the Demon's rage on your brother at the last moment, praise His name."

Clayton nodded his head. "The Prophets of God are first scorned, and then attacked."

We got in front of the hotel, where there was more light, and Clayton took out his handkerchief and began wiping me off. "Brush that suit with a stiff brush once it's dry, Henry, but not before. You can get it to look clean again, but no matter how hard you brush, it's going to stink on rainy days. It's already too tight for you. You better go inside and get it off quick before it shrinks on permanent."

I left them in the street. The landlady gave me my room key and asked me what was wrong. I didn't know what to say, so I just said thank you and went upstairs and into my room. A minute later, she knocked on the door with a basin of hot water and a block of soap and a towel. Before she did anything to help me, she leaned her face close to mine and smelled my breath to see if I had been drinking. I didn't know how to say I had been knocked down, and I didn't want to tell tales, anyway, so I said, "*Je tombe*," which means "I fall."

As I wasn't drunk, she took a little flask of brandy out of her apron and poured me a capful and told me to drink it. It burned so much I thought I might have opened up a cut inside my stomach. She got a screen out of the closet, unfolded it, and made me undress behind it. Then she left. When she came back she had an old robe for me to put on.

When I came out from behind the screen she pointed to my eye and said. "*Oeil poché*." I knew she meant "black eye." Other than that, I didn't look so bad. She emptied all my pockets and put everything under my pillow, put my jacket and pants and shirt on hangers and hung them on a string out the window, and pushed me into the bed. The brandy had made me dizzy, so I just shut my eyes. The last thing I heard, she was locking my door with her passkey. That's when I knew I had picked the right hotel.

In the middle of the night, I felt something working its way down my leg. It was too light to be a rat, and roaches don't walk in straight lines, so I didn't know what it was. I rolled over on my side, and whatever it was pulled back under the bed. I slowly opened my right eye. The moonlight was bright. I didn't see anything, but after a minute I heard somebody wheezing.

I waited some more, and a yardstick rose up beside me. I knew what it was because Mr. Henze and I used one when we had a body that was extra long or extra wide, to see if we would need a special-sized coffin. After the stick was high enough, I grabbed it, and when a head came up behind it, I pulled the stick loose and swung it as hard as I could. The intruder fell back and jumped up and scrambled to the window and stood there with one hand on the sash and the other on his neck. It was the coal thief who had knocked me down in the street. "Please," he said in English, and then, "*Pardon.*"

Then I said, "I play the piano." I wanted to have something over him, and it was the only thing I could think of at the moment. Since "piano" is the same word in French, he knew what I was talking about, probably.

To let him know who was boss, I said, "*Allumez la lampe.*" There was no lamp to light, but he had a match, and he lit it and found a candle. He said "*Pardon*" again, and I could tell he meant it. I had cut him on the neck, and he was bleeding. I got up and gave him my wet towel, which was hanging out the window, and then I said, "*Pourquoi?*" which means "Why?" and he put his hand in his pocket and shook some coins around.

I said, "Deacon George paid you?"

He nodded his head and said "*George, oui*," and then he pointed to his chest. "*Je m'appelle Le Furet.*"

"Like Ferret, the animal?"

He shrugged his shoulders.

I put out my hand. "Henry."

We shook hands. Then he knelt down and took his stick and measured my arms and legs, squinting up at me as if he wanted to remember exactly how I looked. After that he pointed to the bed, went to the window, pulled in my suit and shirt, hung them around his neck, blew out the candle, climbed onto the windowsill, waved, and disappeared straight up.

## CLAYTON COMES TO VISIT MY HOTEL

There's a lot of poultry in cages on roofs in Paris. Being high up, these fowl see the sun when it's still dark down in the street. When the cocks started crowing Wednesday morning, I sat up and looked around. My left eye was puffed almost shut, but I could see out of it, and the other eye was fine. Hanging on the door was a new suit, plus a soft shirt and a blood-red silk cravat. I sat there staring at them while the light got better. Then I went back to sleep.

When I woke up again it was after ten o'clock. The sun was shining in the window. I got up and went to the door and tried my new clothes on. The shirt fit, except for being too big in the neck, which I like. The vest and pants and coat were perfect. There was a square hole in the inside coat pocket, where the former owner's name had been. The whole outfit smelled like perfume.

I heard footsteps coming up the stairs and undressed as fast as I could. Clayton knocked on the door and yelled out, "Henry, you there?"

"I'm coming," I said.

I folded everything up and stuffed it under the bed and opened the door. Deacon George was standing behind Clayton. He had an open jar of black, greasy stuff in his hand. They came in. "We're on an errand of mercy," Clayton said. "Deacon George has some medicine to take down the swelling and keep you from going blind."

"I'm fine," I said. "I don't need anything."

"Where'd you get that old man's robe?"

"My landlady."

"It's ugly. You know that."

"It's fine."

The Deacon dipped three fingers into his black grease, leaned around Clayton, and struck at my eye as quick as a snake. I turned my head away, so most of the stuff went in my ear.

"Don't worry. It's supposed to burn for a while," Clayton said. "That's a sign it's doing its healing work."

I got the wet towel, with Ferret's blood still on it, and wiped off as much as I could. Then I sat down on the bed. If Deacon George came at me again I was going to kick him, and I think he knew it.

Clayton sat down on the chair next to the window. "After we took in last night's offering, the Deacon and I sat up meditating upon your attack. We decided, after all, that the boy was after your life."

"You draw rage upon yourself," Deacon George said. "Your brother, remembering back, says you did that at home when you were little. The sooner you go back there, the better for you."

Clayton got up and opened my valise and took out paper and an envelope and put them on the bed next to me. "Here, so you can write Mama and Papa and say you're on your way. It's best. You've looked upon my success by the seeing of the eyes and the hearing of the ears, as the Scripture says, so you can give true testimony to my power. What happened last night you can skip. Rest today, but make sure you come hear me preaching tomorrow. I'm working on a sermon just for you. Bring the letter to the Chapel and Deacon George will see it's sent, no charge to you. Nothing out of your pocket. Before the day's out, he'll buy you a ticket home."

"No, thank you," I said.

"It's no trouble," Deacon George said.

"When the time comes, I'll do it myself, or ask my friends," I said.

Deacon George looked at me with his beady little eyes. "Friends? Who are they? Where do they live?"

"It's a big city. You'd need a map to find them."

"You must ask the Lord to help you overcome the habit of lying, Henry," Clayton said.

"It's true. I tell a lie every so often, but never about friends," I said.

They left after a while and I took the yellow soap from the

night before and washed off the rest of the salve. Then I wrote Mama and Papa.

*Dear Mama and Papa,*

*I trust this letter will find you in excellent health. I hope the corn is well up by now. When I got here I saw rye (I think), just peeping up in a large field outside the old City wall. The City of Paris is very old, with many beautiful buildings and more big carriages than New Orleans.*

*I am staying at a Hotel. The landlady is very nice. I have seen Clayton three times. He is in excellent health, and sends you his greetings. His Chapel looks like a Church, with everything clean and neat. I heard him preach a sermon last night. He was even more lively and interesting than Reverend Pewbrace.*

*His work here is done, so I am trying to persuade him to go back home.*

*My snakebite is all healed and I am still friends with Dr. Gelineau and his sister Cécile, the people I met on the riverboat down from Saint Louis, and crossed the ocean with. Miss Gelineau has taught me some French. I can sometimes understand some of what people are saying. He is the best of men, and I found out after a storm at sea that she sings. Did I tell you that he is such an excellent Doctor that he teaches other Doctors? I don't think so.*

*Say hello to Oingo for me, and tell her I wish she was*

*here so we could go together and chase French dogs in*
*the park.*

*Your Loving Son,*
*Henry*

I found a post office and mailed it myself, and then I went
to see Dr. Gelineau and Cécile.

# XXXIII

## I VISIT MY FRIENDS AND
## MEET VICTOR HUGO

The front door of Dr. Gelineau's hospital stays open all day and all night, summer and winter. An old Nun sits behind a table inside the door to ask what's wrong with you and summon help. The patients stay on the top two floors, and Dr. Gelineau and the other doctors have rooms on the ground floor.

I told the Nun I wanted to see him. She asked my name, and then she waved her hand to tell me to come closer so she could look at my black eye. The salve had made that side of my face blood red, so I was pretty ugly. While she was looking, I told her that Dr. Gelineau and I were good friends, and that we had gone down the Mississippi River together. She knew the word Mississippi, but she didn't believe I was Dr. Gelineau's friend. Then I said Mademoiselle Cécile had been with us, and she thought for a minute and shook a bell. Right away an old man came. She gave him my name and told him to carry it to Dr. Gelineau.

One of his students, Mr. Robert Devon, from Edinburgh in

Scotland, came out right away and took me down a long corridor to Dr. Gelineau's laboratory. He was standing behind a table with four students. In front of him was a basin of blood with a heart in it. He wiped off his hands and came over and looked at my eye without touching it. "Pull down your cheek. Can you see?"

"Fine."

"How did it happen?"

"I was pushed into the gutter, but I'm fine now."

"No damage?"

"No."

"We will speak about it later. Will you excuse me?" He went back to his table, took the heart out of the basin, and laid it on a piece of white marble. "I must examine this before it turns to *pâté*. Stay and observe if you wish."

He took a scalpel and began his work, talking to the students the way he had talked to me when we were cutting up poor Mr. Brevoort's heart on the boat on the way to New Orleans.

After he was done and washed up, he led his students upstairs to look at some patients, and said I could tag along. We went to four wards. He told each patient to point to where he hurt, lifted up bandages, bent arms and legs, and had the students look into each patient's eyes and feel lumps and feverish places. From time to time he would ask one of them to smell something and say what it was a sign of. They didn't like that duty. I didn't either, when he asked me to do it, but he said that sorting through smells was a big part of a doctor's job.

When we got back to his laboratory he sent his students away to eat. After they were gone, he said, "Your brother is still with his thieves?"

"He doesn't think anything's wrong," I said.

"Then you must keep away from him."

"Not yet," I said.

"Or we must find a way to scatter them."

"How?"

"There is bound to be a solution. That's the American idea, I think? And when he goes home, what will you do?"

"I don't know," I said. "I don't want to leave this soon. Maybe I could find work. I know barrels, and undertaking."

"My sister and I have remarked to each other that you are not without resources. Good. Have you seen her? No? You must. I'll come in a little while. You still have my little map?"

"Yes. In my pocket."

"Go now, and tell her I'll be there soon."

So I went.

On the door of their apartment was a brass knob. When you turned it, five birds in a gold cage inside the apartment jumped up and down and made twittering sounds. I turned the knob once, and the door opened right away. It was Cécile.

"I saw you from the window," she said. "Come in. What happened to your eye? Have you brought it to my brother?"

"He sent me here. I'm fine."

She led me into the living room, which took up the whole front of the apartment, and told me to sit down. There were gold-framed mirrors and pictures on all the walls, little bronze lamps and statues on all the tables, glass cabinets, and vases with flowers in them. As soon as I sat down she asked me what had happened to me. "I was knocked down on the street," I said, "but it was by a friend."

"Oh? One of your brother's thieves?" she said.

"No, he's independent. He didn't hurt me much, and he wouldn't hurt me again. He was sorry he did it as soon as he knew who I was. He brought me an almost-new suit to make peace."

"Your friend is also a tailor?"

"He stole the suit, but only to make it up to me. I don't know who owns it. I don't know what to do with it."

"I would keep it until the owner appears."

"That's what I think, too."

"Are you hungry? Will you take lunch?"

"Yes, thank you."

She went out, and I got up and walked around the room. On the far wall was a big painting of Dr. Gelineau, Cécile, Maurice, and their mother sitting on the red sofa I had been sitting on. It was about ten years old. Cécile was sitting on her mother's lap. Maurice was sitting on the floor in front of her with a toy steam engine in his hand, and Dr. Gelineau was behind the sofa with a book in his hand.

Cécile came back and looked at the picture with me. "After Maurice died, we gave the steam engine to our cousins in Le Havre. Our mother was the most beautiful woman, don't you think?"

"When did you lose her?"

"Five years ago next winter. She was in a coach accident with our father. He was also a physician. Have you proposed to your brother that he should return to America?"

"He doesn't want to go."

"Then you must not allow yourself to become involved with him."

"He's my brother. There must be a way of helping him."

She was still looking at her beautiful mother in the picture. "Think of your parents, left alone in the world without both of you."

The doorbell birds jumped. A servant went to the door and then came back with the message that Dr. Gelineau would be coming with Monsieur Hugo for lunch in ten minutes. I got up to go.

"No, no," she said. "You must not miss Victor Hugo. He is a force of nature. Sit and wait."

A minute later Monsieur Hugo came through the door, with Dr. Gelineau behind him. He was a tall, heavy man. His head was very big and his ears were laid flat against it and pointed at the top. Terriers put their pointy ears back against their heads like that when they fight, so other dogs can't get their teeth into them. He was jumpy like a terrier, too, looking everywhere, sitting down and getting up and walking around and then sitting down again. Every time he sat he would look around to make sure people were watching him.

At first he talked to Cécile, but then she went to look after lunch and he came over and sat down on the sofa next to me and started talking in English. "You are an American," he said. "Dr. Gelineau told me, but I would have seen it. I know everything about America. You are killing the Red Indians. You must put up a monument to these noble people. That's what we would do if we killed them here. And we would write many books about them. Most of them would be idiotic, but mine would be great. What do you think?"

"I don't know," I said. He clapped me on the shoulder and got up again and went out and brought Cécile back from the kitchen, sat down next to her on the piano bench, and gave her a sheet out of his pocket.

"I have recast the Twenty-third Psalm. Now it is a French sonnet. Read it out loud."

While she was reading he went to the bookshelf and took down a French Bible and opened it up, and when she was done he gave it to her and told her to read the Psalm from there. Then he looked at me and asked which one sounded better. I said my French was bad, and besides, my brother was the one in the family who knew the way the Bible should sound.

"Both for music and for idea, mine is better, by a hundred times," he said. "Your brother is a priest?"

"No, Sir. He has a Chapel on rue Lemercier."

"I know that street from end to end. There was a pitched battle there last summer. Excellent people live there. Poor, with great hearts. I know more about the poor people of Paris than the Archbishop, who naturally knows nothing. Your brother has a Chapel for the poor?"

"They're all thieves," I said.

"Of course they are. How else are the poor to live, if not by stealing bread?"

"It's not bread they steal."

"Then I must come and eat some of their cake. I am not the original maker of that idea. Ha ha ha!"

"You should go there some night soon and preach a sermon for the whole street to hear," Dr. Gelineau said.

"Do you think so? Of course. Who better? When does your brother hold forth?"

"Tuesday to Friday at eight, and Sunday morning," I said.

"Today is Wednesday. It might be possible. Everything is possible. I will come and give a speech Friday night. Tell your brother. Every man, woman, and child in the district will press in to hear me. Let the thieves bring their mothers. Thieves have mothers, you know."

"I will ask my brother if Friday is good," I said.

"No no no. Do not ask him. Tell him. Tell him. He will be happy in the end. His Chapel will be famous forever. I know how to lift the spirits of the poor. Two things are required, laughter and rage. I will produce both."

He picked up a gold frame from the table next to his chair, put it in his pocket, looked around the room, smiled, and took it out again. "You didn't see me do that, did you? I would be an excellent thief. Of course, as an honest man, I would always bring the booty back." He looked at it. It was the drawing of me Cécile had made on the boat.

He waggled his finger at her. "When will you draw a picture of me at my work?"

"Today, if you wish," she said.

"I'm too busy today." He put my picture back on the table. Then the servant called us, and we went into the dining room for lunch.

## XXXIV

## I WARN CLAYTON

I said goodbye to Dr. Gelineau and Cécile and Mr. Hugo right after lunch, and went to the Chapel. The front door was locked, but I kept knocking until Clayton heard me and came down and opened it. I could see he didn't want me to come in.

"I'm in the middle of the sermon I'm going to preach for your benefit tomorrow," he said. "The Holy Ghost hates to be broke into, so be quick. How's your eye? It looks fine. The Deacon's salve made the difference, didn't it?"

"I just had lunch with Victor Hugo," I said. "The great French writer?"

"I know who he is."

"He's also a Senator. Everybody in France knows him. He's coming here Friday night at eight o'clock to give a speech."

"No, he isn't, Henry, because I haven't invited him."

"You don't need to invite him," I said. "He's not that kind of man. He just comes, and people flock to hear him."

"Is that all?"

"No. I want to give you a map to keep." I took out the map Dr. Gelineau had drawn for me, and put my finger where he and Cécile lived. "This is for you to hold on to. A friend of mine made it. If you ever need a safe place to go, it's right here, Colyse Street, the number's there. Take it."

"I don't need the kind of friends you have, Henry. Never did, never will."

"Just keep it in case."

"If you promise to go away now so I can do my work, I'll take it."

Without waiting for me to answer, he took the map and slammed the door shut. I was satisfied.

## XXXV

## FERRET'S FAMILY

I went back to my hotel. Ferret was waiting for me in the street. He wanted to show me his family, so I followed him to his alley. There was so much junk there, and the cobblestones were so loose, you had to keep looking down all the time to keep from tripping.

Ferret's family lived on the third storey of a brick building overlooking a courtyard where the alley ended. There were two ways to get up to it, through the front door and up the inside stairs, or up a wooden ladder bolted to the outside of the building. There was a family sitting in front of the front door and spilling out into the street. They waved at Ferret, and they would have been happy to let us through, but they were jammed together, and there was a baby asleep on the top step, and a little girl next to her with a red face, as if she had a fever, so we went up the ladder, Ferret first.

The ladder was pretty good. It had wide steps, and hung out from the wall, so your feet could get a good grip. You had to change ladders halfway up, but a little platform made it easy. The second ladder had a few loose bolts, but there were plenty of tight ones, and the steps were almost new.

There was a door at the top, plus what used to be a balcony. The railing around it was gone, but it was solid. There were two cages on it, with a rooster in one and hens in the other. The door into the building was tied open. Ferret's apartment was the first one on the right. It was one room, with the kitchen part on the left. Ferret's grandmother was standing at the stove, which was really just a heater with a flat top, cutting a turnip into a pot. His father was sitting at a little table drinking some stuff that looked like milk and smelled like licorice. He had his leg up on a chair. Around his foot was a bloody bandage that had fallen down so you could see the running sores between his toes.

Ferret's older sister, Lisette-Claire, was sitting on a bed in the corner by the window. She was bonier than Ferret, with a flat nose and light blue eyes. Next to her, propped up against the wall, was Frère Bernard, who had at one time been a priest, but was now entirely devoted to being Lisette-Claire's particular friend.

It was hotter than midsummer in there, and smoky. The bag of coal Ferret had stolen, or one just like it, was next to the stove. Hanging on the wall over it was my old suit. His grandmother pointed to it and picked up a brush and waved it in the air to show that she had been working on it. It was dry, and the stains were all gone, but the whole front was now brownish green. She climbed up on a broken chair and took it down from the wall and came over to Ferret and held it up against his chest to show me how well it was going to fit.

Ferret kissed her on the forehead and took the suit to hang it back up. As he went by the table, his father tried to grab the suit away from him, but Ferret was too quick and got it on the hook. As he came back, his father made another grab for him. He jumped away, and his father's foot fell off the chair. To judge from the way he screamed and cursed, it must have hurt a lot. Ferret started to lift it back on, and his father kicked him with his good foot, but Ferret kept his balance and threw the foot back on the chair, and the bandage fell off. A cat came out of nowhere, grabbed it in his mouth, and ran out the door with it.

With his father howling and cursing, Ferret tipped half of his licorice drink into a cup and gave it to his grandmother. She had taken a piece of meat out of the box by the window and was pounding it with a wooden hammer, but she stopped long enough to empty the cup in one gulp.

Then Ferret went over to his sister and told her about me. At least, that's what I think he did. She nodded her head and looked at me once, but she was too busy rolling a cigarette to pay much attention. When she was done, she held it up in the air for everybody to see. It was a neat job. Frère Bernard, who had been squinting at me, took it and lit it and began talking about America. Pretty girls could always find work there, he said. It was the only place in the world where a man could be free. He and Lisette-Claire were going to pack up and go there tomorrow or the next day.

I stayed until long after dark. We ate dinner, and afterwards Ferret and I went out onto the balcony and sat there looking down at the street. Lisette-Claire rolled two cigarettes and brought them out to us, and we smoked them. Ferret asked me about America. With the few words I knew, I gave him a pretty good idea of it.

## SPYING ON CLAYTON AND THE DEACON

At midnight, when we knew the thieves would be out stealing, Ferret and I climbed down from his balcony, went to the Chapel, and climbed up to the roof so we could see what Clayton and Deacon George did when the swag came in. We went there the long way around, so we wouldn't have to go by the front door, and when we got to the roof Ferret took some prune cakes out from under his shirt and we ate them.

· The skylight was frosted glass, but it had a hole about the size of a quarter in the bottom left corner, so we could sit with our backs to the wall and just lean forward every once in a while and see if anything was happening. At first the room was empty, with a candle burning in a candlestick on a table in the middle. Clayton and Deacon George were in their rooms sleeping. At least, all the doors were shut and it was quiet. I was glad to see that Clayton had time in the middle of the night to sleep.

Ferret and I kept still because I didn't want to try to talk more French, and we didn't want to make any noise. There wasn't much to do but look up in the sky, where every once in a while you would see a star between the clouds. The moon was high and full, but blurry. I started picking at the slates at the edge of the roof, and after a while one of them broke off and slid down and crashed into the alley. Ferret just shook his head and shrugged his shoulders. In that section of the city things were falling off of buildings and crashing all the time.

Then we heard a noise. Two men came down the alley, went around the corner into the back yard, and opened the door to the back stairs. As soon as they were out of sight, I went to the spy hole and looked. Deacon George must have heard them opening the door, because he was already out of his room and knocking on Clayton's door. Clayton came out with a candle, went over to his worktable, opened the drawer, took out his ledger book, and sat down. Deacon George slid a wooden box out from under the table and sat down next to him. When the thieves came over to them, Clayton already had his pen in his hand and the ledger open.

I couldn't see all the loot the men were taking out of their pockets. It was small items, rings and lockets and such. Deacon George took them in his hand one at a time, looked at them, and dropped them into his box. Then he gave each man some coins out of a pouch, and they went and sat down on beds in the corner.

After that, nothing happened for almost an hour. Clayton was so tired he kept closing his eyes and putting his head down on the book. Deacon George would let him stay that way for a minute, until he was completely asleep, and then poke him and talk to him until he lifted up his head again. It made me think of the cruel Judge who might sit in judgment at Clayton's trial. I could imagine him leaning over his desk waving the ledger book and asking Clayton if the writing was his, and Clayton not knowing what he was saying, and standing silent while the man condemned him.

Just after three o'clock, six thieves came back in a bunch and gave in their booty. Now there were enough men for two card games, and they got to it. We were too high up to see the hands, but it was interesting watching the players bet. Once, when I took a quick look at Clayton's table, Deacon George was sitting by him looking right up into my eyes. After a second he looked away. I was sure, with the dirty frosted glass and the darkness, that he hadn't seen me. We should have left right then, especially as it was starting to drizzle, but I wanted to know what they did when all the thieves were back home, so I stayed where I was. When thief Number Thirteen came back, Deacon George reached up inside the man's coat and snatched out a gold pen and laid it carefully on the table. After he paid him, he went and got an iron box out of his room, unlocked it, and dropped the pen inside.

It was raining harder when the last two thieves came. They dragged their way over to the table and stood there like a pair of rats waiting their turn to drop into the sewer. Ferret and I looked like rats, too, probably, only young instead of old. The last thief had a string of green jewels, with pearls in between. I got a good look at it because Deacon George took out a magnifying glass and held it up to the light. Then he locked it in his lockbox and paid the man, but the man didn't move.

After a minute Deacon George came around the table and whispered in his ear, probably telling him he would give him more money later.

Clayton closed his book and put it in the drawer and went back into his room to go to bed. It was like a daddy and his children. Ferret and I stood up. We were brushing ourselves off when we heard Deacon George scampering up the ladder. He poked his head over the edge of the roof and grinned at me. "*Petit con*" he said, which is a French insult. He stayed there and sang a little song, not in French or English, but in Polish. It had barks and yips in it, so I think it was a hunting song.

Ferret went to the other side of the ladder while he was still singing, and Deacon George came up the last two rungs and stepped down onto the roof. He waved his hand over the edge and looked at me. "Would you care to jump? It's not so far. Yes? No? You are lucky there are two of you. If you had not brought a friend, I would teach you to jump."

I had left the lock of Cécile's hair behind in the hotel, under my pillow, but just thinking about it gave me strength. "You have clouded my brother's mind, and that is an evil thing to do to somebody," I said.

"And you have made a friend of the Ferret. We call him that. *Le Furet*. Do you wonder why? He was the one who knocked you into the gutter last night. You are truly surrounded by assassins."

"He didn't wipe his hands on my shirt," I said.

"That is true. I should have told him to wait and push you in front of a wagon. Boys like him cannot be trusted. You, on the other hand, are a civilized person, a born gentleman, if I may use the term. You voyaged across the Atlantic Ocean to tell your brother something he already knows deep in his heart. Quite a noble record, but now you have made an enemy of me. I am stronger than you, and I am on my own ground, and as long as you stay in this city I can do away with you whenever I wish. Like the Lord, I choose to show mercy at the moment, but I can turn my wrath upon you at any time."

Ferret cursed him and jumped up on the edge of the roof and walked along it, hoping Deacon George would leap at him and give me a chance to get away, but he paid him no attention, telling me to climb down. "We will go visit your brother," he said. "And don't try to run away when you get to the alley. I can outrun the swiftest policeman in Paris, and I can outrun you, and when I knock a man down, he does not get up."

I got to the alley and waited for him. I didn't want to run away and let him tell Clayton stories about me. He grabbed me by the collar and pulled me to the back corner of the building and up the stairs. The thieves were still playing cards. We went into Clayton's room without knocking. Clayton sat up in bed, squinting in the light.

"Your brother has been on the roof all night spying on us through the skylight," Deacon George said.

Clayton shut his eyes. "Henry, you are a disgrace to our family."

Deacon George pushed Clayton's bed with his knee. "Do

you entirely understand what I am telling you, Reverend? Your brother was on the roof spying on us."

"Deacon George hired that boy to knock me down yesterday," I said. "He'd be glad if I was dead."

Clayton put his fingers in his ears and shook his head. "Go home, Henry," he said. "I don't mean back to your hotel, I mean back home, to Missouri. Tell Papa and Mama why I sent you." His eyes were wide-open now. "You always thought you were smarter than me, Henry," he said. "You never said it in so many words, but I could see it in your face, even when you were a baby. Now you see I've got me my own Chapel, and you see men listening to me and saying 'Amen,' and you just can't stand it. It makes you green jealous that I've got to a higher place in life than you. What do you do day and night? You dig graves and clean dead people's toenails. So, I ask you, which one of us has turned out to be the smart one?"

"You can turn one dollar bill into two dollar bills in no time at all, Clayton. I'd never be able to do that."

He smiled. "Well, I'm glad you admit after all these years I know how to be a success. You're a good boy at heart, Henry, except you get these ideas. I want you to promise me right now you'll come listen to my sermon tonight. Miss it, and you'll be putting your soul in danger. And then after that you'll go home."

"I'll come," I said.

"Good boy. Now, go home to bed."

Deacon George pinched my neck hard and let me go, and I

went back downstairs. Ferret met me at the end of the alley and asked what Deacon George had done to me. That gave me a chance to use the word for "neck" that Dr. Gelineau had taught me working on Mr. Brevoort.

I asked him how much Deacon George had paid him to push me down in the street, and he said one franc. I didn't know if that was a fair price or not, but it sounded cheap.

"For a job like that, I think he should have paid you more," I said.

When we were at the hotel I told him that Victor Hugo was coming to Clayton's Chapel at eight o'clock on Friday night, and he should tell everyone about it.

## XXXVII

## CLAYTON DELIVERS A SERMON
## FOR MY BENEFIT

Thursday, I dressed up in my new suit and got to the Chapel early and sat in the back row. When Clayton walked in he stopped next to me and told me to go sit down in the front.

In his prayer, he told God to drive his message like a fiery sword into his brother's heart. Then he picked up his Bible and read from the Gospel of Saint Matthew, Chapter VI, where Jesus teaches the people the Lord's Prayer. When he got to the words "lead us not into temptation," he read them over three times, each time louder than before. Then he closed his Bible, keeping his finger in his place in case he needed to open it up and read it again, and looked at me.

"Beloved Flock," he said, "answer me this question: Who is the bigger sinner, the one who does the sin, or the one who tempts him to do it? Well, Henry? I'm waiting."

"The tempter," I said.

"That's right! The tempter, the tempting one, the one who

tempts, the man or child who behaves temptingly, temptation's pawn."

Now that he had his target, he waited for Deacon George to translate, and then began to talk about different places where woeful and wanton tempters did their wicked work. After that he talked about tempters in the Bible and Roman history, including Satan, who tempted Jesus in the Wilderness, and Brutus, who tempted his friends to murder Julius Caesar, and the Indians, who tempted soldiers to kill them.

"Now, let us turn our attention to Tempters in this dark city, Tempters who do their Perfidious work under our noses." He mentioned Shady Ladies in Pink Petticoats, who tempt weak men to Puff up with Perilous Pride, and Pinch them and Peek at their undergarments, and Prodigal Parasitical Pagan Papists, Praising the Pope and tempting Peasants to copy their Perverse Perfidy.

Then he took a step closer to me, so I had to pull my feet back. "And what would you think, Dear Congregation, if the tempter turned out to be a mere boy? What would you say about him walking into this holy place, wearing a French suit and white silk shirt and red neckcloth, forcing himself upon his kind Elder Brother, claiming that he had crossed the sea only to rescue him, a boy who strutted the streets at night, full of Pride, tempting Pert Poor Persons to Pounce upon him and Push him down onto the Pavement? Would not that Poor Pert Pouncing Person have a right to Punish the boy in Proportion to his Prideful Perfidy?"

By now he had got me to thinking, and I was coming up with other tempters, trappers who tempt minks into traps, and bakers who tempt children into bakery shops, and the Serpent tempting Adam and Eve in the Garden of Eden. In every case, Clayton had it right, the tempters were more to blame than the people they tempted.

An hour later he was done. He said "Amen," and we all said "Amen" back, and he went to the back of the Chapel and stood at the door, the way most preachers do Sunday mornings. Deacon George went and stood next to him. As I shook Clayton's hand I told him he had preached a fine sermon, and reminded him that Victor Hugo was coming the next night.

"Tell him to stay away," Clayton said.

## XXXVIII

## A SPEECH AND A RIOT

When I woke up Friday I decided not to see anybody all day, so I went down to the river and across to the island where the Notre-Dame Cathedral is. After looking around inside for a while, I went the rest of the way to the other side of the river and down to the Champ-de-Mars, to see if the horse races were going. In Paris the horses wear silk shirts, and some of the people in the crowd do too, to match their favorites. I wanted to see that, and how French race-horses ran, but the course was empty. Then I went upriver, past the last sewer drain, to the barges where washerwomen go, and watched for a while.

When I got hungry I went to a *bistro* and had a big meal, and fell asleep at the table. When I woke up I looked at the newspapers that they kept on sticks on the wall, but all I could think of was Mr. Hugo's speech coming, so I went back to my hotel. On the way I stopped to see if the Chapel was open. It wasn't, and it was dark inside.

By nightfall, when I left my room and went back to the

Chapel, the street was full of people. I saw two thieves from Clayton's Flock moving around looking for pockets to pick, and for sure there were other thieves I didn't know. Ferret had climbed onto the iron bar where Clayton's sign hung, and was standing on it in my old suit. Across the street was a newspaper artist with a block of paper and three pencils, drawing the scene. It was a good picture, but he put a straw hat on Ferret that made him look like a farmer just arrived in the city. Clayton was standing in the second-floor window banging on the glass and yelling at Ferret to get down. The artist drew the window open, with Clayton leaning out of it and looking up the street for Mr. Hugo.

I went through the crowd and down the alley and kept knocking on the back door until Clayton came down and let me in. He stood on the bottom step with his hand on the wall. "You've already seen the upstairs twice," he said. "You don't need to see it again."

"I don't want to. I just want to get into the Chapel for when Mr. Hugo comes."

Clayton shook his head. "You know what you've been to me since the day you were born, Henry? A blight, that's what you've been. My whole Flock is grieving because they can't hear me preach tonight. Deacon George tells me that's how they all feel, but do you care? Not a bit! I still have two more Commandments to preach on, and I have to skip a night. It's not right, Henry."

"I'm sorry, Clayton. I didn't invite him, truly. You're a better preacher than he is, any day. Everybody knows it. But your Flock is all thieves, and if you get arrested, the Judge is going to think you're the biggest thief of all. You got to get away. Go preach in Saint Louis, where people can understand what you're saying to them."

"You want to talk about thieves, Henry? All right, I'll talk about thieves. Let's say one or two of my True Believers steals something small every once in a while, taking from the rich to help the poor. They're still sheep of my Flock, and I'm their shepherd. They have to hear my voice every day. If they stray and don't come back to me, you'll be to blame. Go on in the Chapel if you like, but nobody else comes in until I unlock the door and let them."

He went upstairs, and I went into the Chapel. The lanterns weren't lit yet, so I found a match and did it, and then I lined up the chairs better and went to the front door. There were people with their faces right up against the window, hoping to be the first ones in. The people behind them were either looking down the street for Mr. Hugo's carriage, or up at Ferret.

After a minute there was a shout, and then a roar that kept getting louder all the time, and the crowd began squeezing together to let the carriage through. The driver stopped as close to the Chapel as he could, and two big footmen cleared the people from right in front of the door. Then Victor Hugo was standing on the top step of the carriage and waving to the crowd. Most of them were on the far side and couldn't see him, but they cheered like everyone else. Right and left in the carriage windows I could see Dr. Gelineau and Cécile.

Clayton came up behind me with a key in his hand and

pushed me aside. "Get out of my way so I can greet him. What's his name again?"

"Victor Hugo."

"Right. I know that." He opened the padlock and pulled it off and kicked the door until it opened.

Victor Hugo came in, with Cécile and Dr. Gelineau behind him. Then there was a flood of people, men, ladies, old women, children in rags with no shoes, mothers, and even the girl who sold ribbons and shoelaces. Dr. Gelineau saw me as he went by and reached out to grab my hand, but the shoving was too great, so he just put Cécile between himself and the wall and the crowd pushed them along toward the front. Clayton was right behind him, holding on to his coat.

In less than a minute, all the seats were gone and there was no room left to stand. I climbed up onto the back windowsill, where there were already two men and a boy. Cécile and Dr. Gelineau were in the corner, which was good because it was near the back door. She was talking to a woman with two babies, one of them crying, and Dr. Gelineau was near the altar, getting somebody to stand up to let a very old lady sit down.

Mr. Hugo was standing next to the altar, looking twice as big as anybody. He pushed back the crowd and made the ones standing in front sit down on the floor. Then he held up his hands and it was quiet except for the one baby crying. He went over to it and whispered in its ear, and it stopped.

Clayton stepped in front of the altar to welcome everybody and introduce him, but Mr. Hugo started to speak right away, and Clayton had to go in back of the altar and stand there. At first Mr. Hugo walked back and forth talking, the same way he had done at the Gelineaus', but then he came to rest in the middle and gave his speech standing still.

He spoke loudly and slowly, saying the same words over and over. He was for liberty, brotherhood, and equality, he said, and against greedy bankers who hated the people and loved only gold, and all judges, and jailers, and Senators who took bribes. From time to time he would stop talking with his arm up in the air, and we would all clap and yell and stamp our feet so hard it made the whole place shake. During the cheer at the end of his speech, the man next to me jumped up and down so hard he put his foot through the window.

People began to chant *"Li-ber-té! Li-ber-té!"* Mr. Hugo tried to step over to the corner where Cécile and Dr. Gelineau were, but as soon as they saw that he was trying to leave, the people rushed him and picked him up and carried him down the center aisle to the door. Eight policemen were waiting there to help him get back in his carriage, which made the people mad. When he was in his carriage, the policemen pushed their way back in, bottling us inside. I yelled, probably in English, to tell them to go protect Cécile, but nobody could hear anything for the screaming.

The policemen looked at the angry crowd, then looked at each other, and then backed up and went outside again, and the people began to push their way through the door. Somebody grabbed at my shoe, probably just to have something to hold on to, and I fell down on him. I climbed back up and looked to see if Cécile was safe. There was a little more room in front now. Dr. Gelineau was talking to an old lady sitting on a chair fanning herself, and Cécile was standing in the corner with the mother of the little babies. She had one in her arms. The two women looked like old friends stopping to talk in the park.

Suddenly a man from Clayton's flock came up to Cécile and tried to take the baby from her, hoping the police would leave him alone if they thought he was a father. She shook her head and turned away from him. When he reached around to grab the baby she bent down, picked up a broken chair leg, swung it through the air, and hit him on the top of the head. He just looked at her, with blood running down his face, so she swung it again, harder, and he dropped like a stone. Dr. Gelineau stepped on him, and Cécile and the old lady and the mother with the babies went out the back door, behind Clayton.

I stayed in the windowsill until the place was empty. Then I went upstairs to the second storey. It was dark, but there was moonlight coming down through the skylight, so I could see where things were. This was my chance to get rid of Clayton's ledger. I opened the drawer of his desk and took it out. Just then, somebody threw a stone through the front window, and the noises on the street got twice as loud. I went to the window and peeked out. Ferret was on the iron post again, swinging a lantern back and forth and leading a chant, but instead of *"Li-ber-té! Li-ber-té!"* he was shouting *"Bar-ri-cade! Bar-ri-cade!"*

I sat down against the wall, with the ledger under me because of the glass on the floor, and waited. After a while I heard policemen on horses coming, and I prayed that Ferret would be quick enough to get down and run away. The chanting stopped. Now it was just yelling and screaming. Then there were shots, not many, and everything got quiet. I went into Clayton's room and climbed under the bed and kept still, trying to decide the best way to destroy the ledger.

## I DESTROY EVIDENCE

I thought about burning up the ledger one page at a time, but I was afraid somebody on the street might see the light and call the police. At midnight, I came out of Clayton's room. My idea was to wait by the broken window until one o'clock. I sat on the floor and watched mice for a while, slowly lifting up my head from time to time and peering out the window. A woman was going around on the street picking up things that had been dropped and putting them in a bag. At the end of Ferret's alley, people were building a barricade. I had never heard it being done before but I knew that's what it was.

When the church bells struck one I stood up and started to walk across the room. Then I heard a man coming up the stairs. I put the ledger under my shirt, went into Clayton's room, closed the door most of the way, and stood still watching through the crack. The door at the top of the stairs opened, and Deacon George came in. He stood for a minute listening, and then he went to his room and got out the iron lockbox and brought it over to the table and opened it and felt around inside. I could hear the jewelry clinking. He locked it again and went back to the stairs, and I figured I was free, but I must have moved and made a noise, because he turned around slowly and looked my way.

I pulled my door open, yelled "Fire!," and ran straight at him. If I had done anything else, he would have cornered me and tried to kill me, but with the steep stairs behind him he jumped out of the way, and I was past him and halfway down, going three steps at a time, before he could reach out to grab me. As soon as I hit the bottom I bolted across the back yard, went over the fence, jumped over boxes and cans to get to the next street, turned left, toward the river and the lights on the Champs-Elysées, where there were always peo-ple, and ran as hard as I could.

He had not lied about being able to run fast, but we were both crippled by what we were carrying. The ledger was bouncing against my belt, pulling my shirt out of my pants, so I had to put my hands under it to keep it from falling out, and he had his iron box full of jewelry he didn't want to lose. My feet were slapping on the cobblestones, and there was wind in my ears, but even then I could hear the jewelry bang-ing against the lid every step he took. And he was growling the way he did that night when I flipped the maggots onto his trousers.

After two blocks, he stopped and yelled at me. "I have something from your brother."

I stopped and turned around. He was about half a block away, and breathing hard.

"Truly, I do," he said. "He wants you to have it."

He started to walk toward me, and I started to back up. Still, he was going a little bit faster than I was.

"Where?"

"At your friends' apartment. He has your map." He put his hand in his pocket. "He gave me a copy. Shall I tell you when he wants to meet you? He says it is of the greatest possible importance."

I stopped backing up. "When?"

"Does he know your friends yet? He didn't tell me."

"No."

"You are very fortunate to have them. That is a great skill, making friends, wouldn't you say?"

I didn't answer him.

"Modesty becomes you. You're quite a charming boy. But you know that, don't you? You must. Of course you do."

My heart was pounding and I knew I should run, but it was as if my shoes were nailed to the stones.

"He doesn't know them," I said. "Don't come any closer."

"I would stop, as you say, but I don't want people to think we're going to stay here and keep them from sleeping."

Just then a window opened above my head and somebody yelled something, and I jumped, and started running again. A knife went by over my head. I wondered if he had a pistol, but I could hear him behind me, so I thought he probably didn't. We were a block from the bright lights on the Champs-Elysées, with carriages going back and forth. Then, suddenly, I was in the lights and among the horses. I saw two policemen walking along on the far sidewalk, between the street and the river, and started to run toward them, but then I thought of the ledger in my shirt and turned back, ducking between two fast carriages, hitting the second horse's nose and just missing the back of a carriage going the other way. Deacon George, right behind me, got caught between that carriage and the one behind it, and went under the wheels. I flew up a side street, and when I came to a sewer, I stopped. It was silent. I was alone.

The main streets in Paris have the best sewers in the world. With nobody in sight, I sat down on the curb, took the ledger out from under my shirt, and opened it up. On the front page, in the space where you put your Company's name, Clayton had written "THE REVEREND DOCTOR W. CLAYTON DESANT" and, under it, "Book of Gifts and Offerings." The first twenty-seven pages were full, and he had started page twenty-eight. He had his signature at the bottom of all but the last one. I ripped the pages out one by one, looking up and down the street in between to be sure I was still alone, tore them into tiny pieces, and dropped them in the sewer. After I was done, with seventy-two clean pages left, I decided to keep the book and write a record of this adventure in it, but only if I got Clayton safely home to America.

## XL

## IN THE CITY LATE AT NIGHT

I put the ledger back under my shirt and went to Dr. Gelineau's building on the rue Colyse. The downstairs door had an iron gate pulled down, but I didn't want to go inside, anyway. I went across the street and climbed up into the big chestnut tree. Dr. Gelineau was awake, standing on the little balcony and smoking a cigar, so I knew that Cécile was safe in bed. He was watching the sky, and he didn't notice me.

I stayed in the tree for over an hour, wondering where Clayton was. I knew Deacon George had been lying about him coming here, but that didn't tell me where he was. He didn't have any friends, except thieves, so where would he go now to lay his head? If he still had my money in his pocket, he could have rented a room in the best hotel in Paris, but I knew he hadn't done that. Maybe he was sitting in the railroad station, or already on a train to Le Havre. Wherever he was, at least there was nothing on paper that could be used as evidence against him anymore, and what thief would come out of hiding to accuse him to the police?

Around three, I got hungry. One day on the ship, Cécile had told me about Les Halles, the farmers' market in Paris, and I thought there must be places near it where the farmers ate after they had unloaded their goods, so I went there. The sight of blood never puts me off my food, so I took the long way around, crossing the Champs-Elysées to see how much blood Deacon George had lost. I found a big stain, and some of it had splattered, so I figured he was dead. It made me glad. I went to Les Halles and ate rolls and hardboiled eggs and drank coffee.

## XLI

## INSIDE A BOTTLE

I wanted to find Ferret before daylight, so after eating I went to the barricade, getting there about four-thirty, with the first light in the sky. The barricade was high and wide enough, but it was in the wrong place. No matter how strong they are, barricades can't stand up to cannons, so you need to build them on open streets, with other streets and alleys going off. That way, you can escape when they get blasted down. One built at the end of a closed-off alley is like a cork in a bottle.

There were two policemen standing next to the building across from it, so I just walked there slowly and stood looking at it for a while. It was made out of wooden boards, bricks, wheelbarrows, pieces of machinery, old wagons tipped on their sides, and at least two brass beds. One end was anchored by an iron axle, and the other by a piano. An old man with a rifle and a bottle of wine sat on a chair on top of it, smoking his pipe.

The policemen didn't even look at me. Their job was to arrest whoever came out, so they just shrugged their shoulders when I said I wanted to climb in and find my friend. The old man on the chair saluted me going over. The barricade looked neater on the people's side. On the ground behind the piano a man was sleeping on his back with his sword on his chest.

There were some men around a fire on a grate halfway between the barricade and the end of the alley, smoking and drinking. They looked at me, but they didn't seem to mind that I was there. I went up the two ladders to Ferret's apartment. The rooster on the second landing was already cocking his head at the first light, but I woke up the hens. I stayed there a minute talking to them, and when I stood up I heard the sound of iron wheels and marching soldiers coming along the rue Lemercier. I stayed there until I saw the cannon and the caisson and the soldiers, and then I went into the hall.

Ferret's door was open, and there was a candle burning in the room, so I didn't have to feel my way there. He and his father were sitting next to each other. His father was showing him how to load a two-trigger, two-barrel pistol. Ferret still had on my old suit and shirt, plus a red-white-and-blue cravat. He looked like a gentleman who had been awake all night and was now getting ready to fight a duel. His father turned the gun barrel down over the table, and one of the balls dropped out. He picked it up and drove it back in with a matchstick.

Ferret's grandmother was stirring something on the stove. She came over to the table and grabbed Ferret's cravat and stroked it. "*Drapeau de la Révolution Française,*" she said, which means "Flag of the French Revolution." She asked me if I wanted to have some bread and wine, but I told her I had eaten at Les Halles. After a while, Ferret put the gun in his belt upside down. I told him it was pointing to his head, but he didn't mind. Neither did his father. The rooster crowed. He shook his father's hand, kissed his grandmother, waved to his sister and her special friend, who were asleep, and we left and went down the ladder. Halfway down, while we were changing ladders, the gun slipped out of Ferret's belt and fell down onto the cobblestones and went off. With the echo, there was no way of telling if both barrels had fired or not.

When we got down we set about looking for it. I stepped on it right away. I didn't want to tell him I had found it, because I knew the soldiers would be harder on people with guns, but then I picked it up and gave it to him anyway. Both triggers were sprung, so he hid it under some rags.

It started raining. We went to the barricade. The old man was still sitting on his chair on top of the piano, looking down on the soldiers. The men who had been around the fire, plus some others, talked to Ferret, and two of them, who were drunk, danced with each other. Nobody seemed mad at Victor Hugo, who had started the trouble and was now safe at home in bed.

There was a cannon pointed at the barricade, but everything was so peaceful and easy that we climbed on it to see what was happening along the street. The soldiers were standing at the corner with their guns stacked under oilcloth to keep them dry, so we knew they were loaded and primed. It was as if their side and our side had made a secret pact not to shoot, or throw things, or curse at each other, or even make a sound.

If our side had wanted to draw blood, we could have done it. We had a few rifles, and plenty of stones, and a barricade to hide behind for the first volley. Of course, everybody knew that we were bound to get beaten in the long run. So why didn't we surrender? Because none of us wanted to go back home without doing *something*. If you live in a city where the police can come at night and arrest you, charge you with being a revolutionary, and send you off to Algeria, you get to hate them so much you can't think straight, so you take foolish risks.

The Sergeant ordered his soldiers to uncover their rifles and shoulder them and march back and forth, and when they did, we began to shout at them. Two wives, each one with a child, came across the courtyard to call their husbands inside, but the men said mean things to them and sent them away. The drunk sleeping with the sword woke up and started singing a song, but one man told him to shut up because it was an Army song from the old Monarchy.

Then a girl about twelve years old opened her window on the third floor and began to call down at the soldiers, inviting them to get out of the rain and come up to her room and take off their uniforms so she could iron them flat. The Sergeant moved most of his men half a block up the street, leaving four behind, knowing that the next thing coming out of that window might be boiling water. The four men trimmed the aim of the cannon, which was a twenty-four-pounder, so it was pointing straight at the center of the barricade.

They loaded it with powder, and rolled the ball into it. The ball was so heavy they had to use a sling to get it in. Ferret and I started to climb down, but a man at the other end of the barricade told us to stay where we were because the cannon was too close to fire without hurting everybody on both sides.

The Sergeant saw the same thing, and ordered his men to roll up a twelve-pounder, wedge it between the caisson and the twenty-four-pounder, and aim it. Even a twelve-pounder was dangerous to everybody in such a tiny space, so he sent his men around the corner to hide, put in a long fuse, lit it, and ran away. Ferret and I just stayed where we were as if it were a game. One of our men climbed over the barricade and ran to the cannon, pulled the fuse out and threw it on the ground. It landed in a puddle, but it kept burning. Then the Sergeant came back cursing, picked it up, and stuck it in the twenty-four-pounder.

Ferret and I jumped down and ran as fast as we could to a cellar halfway back on the right side and fell in on top of some men who had been there all the while. They kindly made room for us. The cannon didn't go off, and didn't go off, and didn't go off, and I began to think the fuse had gone out. A man in a doorway across from us started running our way, to get better shelter, and then came the explosion.

It was a big noise. A heavy rain of splinters and stones and bits of machinery came down on us, plus brick dust, which stuck to us because we were wet. The man crossing the courtyard got a tabletop across his chest from armpit to armpit. It was all he could do to breathe while he bled to death against the wall. It took less than a minute. Other men were limping around, not knowing where to go, and the old man who had been on top of the barricade was sitting on the street halfway back. He didn't have a scratch, but there was an iron wheel on his foot.

The soldiers ran in through the smoking hole, yelling, put us in a circle, and made us sit down on the wet street. Some of them had been covered with dust, too. After a minute they stood us up and searched us, and then they made us sit down again. Then they put us to work sorting what was left of the barricade into two piles, things you could burn, like chairs and doors and loose boards, and things you couldn't, like brass beds and wheels. Then the Sergeant ordered us all to piss on the pile that couldn't be burned, in front of everybody, and set fire to the other, and sit down again. It had stopped raining, but everything was soaked and the fire was smoky.

I saw Dr. Gelineau coming through what was left of the barricade with his big surgery bag. He went straight to the old man with the wheel on his foot. At first I didn't know if he had seen me, but after he had sawed the man's foot off and tied the blood vessels, he stood up and looked directly at me and nodded. Then he spoke to the Sergeant and asked to see me, but the Sergeant was still angry and he wouldn't let him do it.

## XLII

## WE SPEND A NIGHT IN THE
## SAINT-LAZARE PRISON

They marched us to jail two by two. I told Ferret when we started off that Dr. Gelineau would figure out how to get me out of the prison, and I would find a way to take him with me. Then I asked him what his real name was.

"Paul Eugène," he said.

"*Le Furet est mort*," I said, which means "The Ferret is dead."

"*Mort et bien mort*," he said, which is the same as saying "Dead as a doornail."

Everybody was tired, including the soldiers, so it was a slow walk. People along the way stopped and stared at us, but nobody shouted at us or threw anything. One old man clapped his hands as we went by. After we crossed the place de l'Europe and were starting down rue de Paradis, I saw Clayton coming along the street toward us. He was studying Dr. Gelineau's map. As soon as he saw me he turned around and stood with his back to us, looking in a bookstore window.

I didn't blame him. There was nothing he could have done to help.

When we got to the prison the soldiers kept us outside the big wooden doors and took down our names. Then they took us inside to a big hall, like a ballroom, lined us up facing the wall, searched our clothes again, and left us with one guard. The only sweet smell in the whole prison was wet plaster, so I didn't mind having my nose next to it. Because Ferret and I had been walking and talking together, they could see we were friends, so they put us in different cells. I went into Cell Fourteen, and he went into Cell Fifteen, across the hall.

My cell had a little window facing north high up in the wall. There wasn't much to see there, anyway. There were seven other men. As soon as they found out I was an American, they were friendly and asked questions. One of them had a brother in Baltimore, Maryland.

Every time I heard the iron door at the end of the hall open, I watched for the cell door to open and Dr. Gelineau to walk in. Night fell, and he still didn't come, but I didn't worry. I had decided what I would say when he walked through the door. I would pretend I was a student doctor and he was my teacher, and I would yell out, *"Ici, Docteur! Henri Desant, votre étudiant!"*

They fed us an early dinner. It was some sort of soup and a piece of bread. When they collected the pot and spoons, the cell became dark. I began to worry that they might come in the morning and send me to another prison before Dr. Gelineau figured out how to get me free. I was sure Ferret was downhearted, so I was sorry we were not together. There were only six cots in the cell, and they were already spoken for, but I was so tired I fell asleep sitting up in the corner. Twice during the night they put a new man in with us. Each time, I woke up thinking it was either Dr. Gelineau come to get me, or the jailers come to take me away.

Morning came and they brought us salty water and a dipper, plus bread. Then, after ten, our cell door opened and Dr. Gelineau, Mr. Hugo, the Superintendent of the Prison, and a jailer came in. The Superintendent was wearing a little square hat. He had three medals on his chest, and he called Mr. Hugo "Senator." I waved my hand in the air and said my short speech.

Dr. Gelineau came over to me, kissed me on both cheeks, squeezed my arms, looked at the Superintendent, and told him what a good student I was. Then he flicked something alive out of my hair and said I would have to take a bath before he would let me examine patients again.

Mr. Hugo dragged the Superintendent over to me and told him what promising students Americans were, and that my brother, the Reverend Doctor W. Clayton Desant, was waiting outside in the carriage and would be glad to see me.

I then mentioned "*votre étudiant Paul Eugène*," saying he was waiting in Cell Fifteen, across the hall.

Dr. Gelineau slapped his forehead and looked at Mr. Hugo as if he had just remembered his other student.

Mr. Hugo leaned into the Superintendent's face and told him he knew it was not his fault that two excellent students of the great Dr. Gelineau, from the Hospital of Saint-Jean, had been wrongly jailed, and that they had to be let go immediately.

The Superintendent shook his head and showed him a paper with our names on it.

Mr. Hugo said he had already seen it, and that it was almost perfect, except for its errors. He took the paper, crossed out my name and Ferret's, and signed it in both places. Then he gave the paper back, put his arm on the Superintendent's shoulder, and pushed him toward the door.

We went out of the cell, Mr. Hugo and the Superintendent leading, and over to Cell Fifteen. In half a minute Ferret was in the hall, blinking. Then Mr. Hugo took the lead in getting us out, but he didn't know his way, so we were soon up against a wall. He laughed, turned the Superintendent around as if he had been making a joke, and let him lead us out.

There was a carriage parked across the street, in front of a slaughterhouse. Mr. Hugo kissed the Superintendent on both cheeks and said goodbye, and we crossed the street and climbed into the carriage. Cécile and Clayton were sitting there waiting with bread, cheese, and wine. As soon as the door was shut, Dr. Gelineau rapped on the ceiling with his cane and we drove away at a gallop. As we were going around the first corner I thanked him. "No, no," he said. "I have to protect my students." Mr. Hugo waved his hand in the air. "I found the Superintendent to be charming a man," he said. "He deserves all of his medals."

Clayton punched me in the arm. "The Doctor here is going to put us up at his house. So, you see, everything works out for True Believers like me."

I nodded my head. I was looking at Cécile's hand with the heart-shaped freckle. I wanted to bend over and kiss it, but of course I didn't.

## XLIII

## TWO OF US LEAVE PARIS

Ferret had to get out of Paris right away. The police would never arrest Senator Victor Hugo for preaching to the poor, but Ferret, whose name was known, had kept the riot going, so the police were bound to come for him again. We decided he should leave for America right away, and I wrote a letter to Mama and Papa for him to carry along.

*Dear Papa and Mama,*

*I am fine. Here is my friend Paul Eugène. As you will see, he does not speak English, but he is very smart and will soon learn it, and then he can tell you about some of our times together.*

*He has a heart of gold, and he is a true friend. He longs to be honest, but do not put temptation in his way.*

*Now that I think of it, he may decide not to come to you, so you may never see this letter about him. I hope you do, but if not, Paul knows best.*

*I will write you again soon. I hope Clayton will be*
*back soon, too. His work here is done.*

*Your Son,*
*Henry*

In the afternoon, Cécile and I went to the hospital and got Ferret some pants and shirts out of the room where they put the clothes of men who die with no families, and put them in a valise. We left the stinking suit there to be burned.

After dinner, Dr. Gelineau and Cécile and I went to the train station and saw Ferret off to Le Havre. I was going to give him my French Bible to take along, but I remembered at the last minute that he didn't know how to read. I wanted to split what was left of my money with him, but Dr. Gelineau had already given him enough, and wouldn't let me. I was sad to say goodbye to him, but it was for the best.

The next day after lunch, Clayton and I went for a walk in the park. I told him what I had done with his ledger, and that Deacon George had died chasing me. He took the news very calmly. "The Lord gives and the Lord takes away," he said. "The Deacon's death is a great loss, especially for you. You would have become the best of friends. But do not mourn, Henry. He is in Heaven with the other Saints now."

"It's enough to make you think," I said.

Clayton pulled himself up to his full height and looked at me. "Think? Think? About what?"

"About not letting people flatter you."

"You were the one flattered, Henry. You flattered yourself

into great foolishness is what you did. You read my letter and flew over here thinking to save me. I never needed saving. You was the one needed saving. I was fine."

"I guess some people never learn," I said.

"Take that lesson to heart, Henry, and I'll be satisfied," Clayton said.

I asked him what he wanted to do next.

"Me? I am praying about that question right now. I have done God's will in Paris, as any fool can plainly see. Now I must find a fresh field of service. I will eat in solitude tonight, in thoughtful prayer, and tomorrow at breakfast I will announce my new calling."

"Dr. Gelineau is taking me to the hospital early."

"Then I will make God wake me up even earlier."

The next morning he was at the table eating when the rest of us got there. "Doctor," he said, "answer this question: What does the Lord want for His People?"

"If I were the Lord, I would want to see all men happy and healthy," Dr. Gelineau said.

"Two-thirds complete, Doctor, two-thirds. He wants us to be happy, healthy, *and successful*. He wants us to be rich in the goods of the world. And He has shown this Great Truth to me, W. Clayton Desant. I see with crystal clarity that He wants me to be successful. And everybody else who can see that and take advantage of it. Let me tell you a story. The day they took Henry to prison, I saw him coming with his ragtag gang of peasants, and a miracle happened. God prompted me to turn my back to him and look in the window of the store behind me. And what sort of store was it? A bookstore. And what was in the window of that bookstore? A whole shelf of books, in matching leather bindings, called *Encyclopedias*, or some such. Each book has a different letter of the alphabet."

"*Encyclopedia*," Cécile said.

"Right, little lady. That's the ticket. Tells everything about everything?"

"Everything we think we know so far," Dr. Gelineau said.

"A good idea, in its way, but nobody needs to know that much. Nobody. It would take all day to find one fact in all that pile."

"We have one in the music room," Cécile said. "They are quite easy to use."

Clayton smiled at her. "You are a female, Miss Gelineau, and therefore you skip around from letter to letter, not knowing what you need to know. God gave you a father and a brother to tell you. I am going to write an *American* Encyclopedia. It will have all the facts people need, in plain down-to-earth American English."

"A simple idea," Dr. Gelineau said.

"Thank you, Doctor. And here's where you come in. You draw me a picture of the body, and I'll put it smack in the middle of the book, with your name underneath of it. You'll be famous."

"I can draw simple maps," Dr. Gelineau said, "but drawing the anatomy of a human being is very complicated."

"You know the trouble with you, Doctor? You think like a Frenchman. Just draw me the bones and the muscles, and maybe the brain, plus parts like the eyes, things like that. None of the parts that would make a lady blush or ask the wrong questions."

"You would leave parts out?"

"Why not? If God had wanted us to see everything inside of us, he would have put windows in our bellies."

"It is an interesting project, but I think you should find someone else to do the drawing."

"Suit yourself. I could do it myself, probably. Just copy what I want out of a doctor book. It won't be one of these long Frenchie books, not a bit of it. Maybe one hundred and twenty pages. What counts is selling it. I'm going to recruit myself an army of hardworking young men, with good characters, to knock on every door south to New Orleans and east to New York. It's got to be colorful, with all the knowledge a man could possibly use. Who could say no to a book like that? I got to working on the letter 'A' during the night. It will have four pages, one for 'Aches,' one for 'Agriculture,' one for 'Apostle,' and one for 'Alabama.' I haven't decided on a price yet. That book you wrote about me, Henry, what did the customers pay? Two cents a page?"

I told him I didn't remember.

"Two dollars including cardboard covers, let's say, and I'm bound to sell a hundred thousand in the first year. I leave it to you to do the multiplication. I'll call it *Everyman's Universal Encyclopedia and Medical Guide,* by the Reverend Doctor W. Clayton Desant. Being a Doctor on the front of a book never hurt anybody, as I'm sure you know, Doctor."

"I've never written one."

"No? Get cracking on one, I say. It's the short cut to success. I'm not just thinking about myself. I'm thinking about Henry, here, too. Blood is thicker than water, as I'm sure you will testify, ha ha ha. So here's my offer to him, made before witnesses: six months as a salesman, and if he does well, he can have the entire state of Missouri."

"I'm staying here," I said.

"What for, when I'll be gone?"

"I'll find work."

"At what? Never mind. Suit yourself."

The next day, he left for home.

## XLIV

## APRIL 1851, MY LIFE IN PARIS

It is now two years since I arrived in Paris. I keep busy. Four nights a week I do janitor work for the Nuns, and days I study medicine under Dr. Gelineau. The janitor work is easy, just cleaning and carrying.

Papa and Mama are still on Aunt Minna's farm in Rocheport. They plan on coming to visit me sometime, but the best season for crossing the ocean is also their busiest time. Ferret helped them with the harvest in the fall of 1849, but he left for San Francisco as soon as the barn was full. I know I will get a letter from him someday, as soon as he learns to read and write, or he will walk into the hospital with his pockets stuffed with California gold.

I go see his grandmother and his father on the first Sunday of every month. His father still has the running ulcers on his toes. They won't get any better as long as he drinks what he does. I go past the Chapel on my way there. It's a tavern again, called L'Evangéliste Américain. Business is good.

Every time I see the signpost, I think of Ferret standing on it waving his lantern and stirring up the crowd.

Clayton got home with no trouble. Six months later he sent me this letter:

*Dear Henry!*

*Great News!!!* Everyman's Universal Encyclopedia and Medical Guide: The Ancient Secrets of Eternal Health Revealed! *written and illustrated by the Reverend Doctor W. Clayton Desant, is selling like ice in July!!*

*By the way, as I can tell you now, I knew from the first that Deacon George was evil. My plan was to lure him home to the U.S. of A. and call the police as soon as his feet touched our sacred soil. You ruined my plan, Henry, like you often have in the past, but as your* Elder Brother, *I forgive you. That is the sort of man I am!*

*More Good News!!! Clemmy Burke has consented to be my wife. Do you think we will have our Honeymoon in Paris? NEVER. Ha ha.*

*Papa and Mama are fine, the last I heard. If you want to come home and sell books, I can let you have as many as you want, up to a certain number, below the usual price, because you are family.*

*Sincerely,*
*Your Brother, Clayton*

*P.S. Why are you there with them, when you could be
here with me? Think it over.*

I wrote back wishing him good luck.

Dr. Gelineau is in excellent health, teaching students and
helping people get well, and Cécile is perfect. There are two
rich old men mooning over her and sending her flowers, but
neither one has made a declaration yet, so she can't send
them away. She gives me dinner one or two times a week. We
talk French and English both. My French still makes her
laugh sometimes.

My task is to learn what Dr. Gelineau has to teach. I will
never know as much about the human body as I need to
know, but he says I'm making good progress, and since he
knows more about the Spark of Life than anyone else in the
world, I guess it must be so. I am at home here. No one could
ask for more.